HE LIVES BLUE

By Marissa St. Clair

Table of Contents:

THE RALLY
Chapter 1

O N his way from a construction site not too far away from his apartment, Sam's pickup truck accelerated in the lit up streets of downtown Manhattan the light was changing from green to amber, "I can catch it", he said with a scarce grin as he held the wheel tight and flew past the light. The autumn air seeped into his truck's cabin. He was almost home and couldn't wait to see Ruby. He had met her online years back as she was going to school to be a teacher. She was living on campus but came to stay over at his place most of the time.

Sam was not in love with her, he was not ready for a full-blown relationship, every time it came up in their conversations he would detour to another subject, which Ruby hated.

He pulled up to his parent's luxurious brownstone in Brooklyn.

One of his neighbour's walked up to his own apartments while, Sam parallel parked his truck.

"I remember when you guys first moved in, his neighbor sounded uncanny, this place was a disaster, owned by crack heads and squatters."

"Yeah, my parents fixed it up great, right?" Sam replied walking to his front door.

"Yupp." His neighbor said going inside.

Sam's dad and mother purchased it after they sold some of their land in South Carolina.

The brownstone had red paint on its newly renovated structure with a brass knocker to compliment the door.

Sam stuck the key in the bottom basement door and opened it to a furnished apartment space where his Dad set him up. There was a kitchen, two bedrooms, living room, and a breakfast nook.

His mom had agreed with him before she passed away from cancer that this would be his apartment.

A sense of her would be around him every time he walked through his doors. His mom was different then his dad, she went out of her way to help and support more impoverished communities especially during holidays.

His father who use to be a police officer was not all too helpful.

Sam hopped in the shower getting all his important parts then hopped out drying himself off with the freshly washed towel that his maid, Wanita folded that morning.

She cleaned only his section of the house as it always smelt fresh every day when he walked through the doors.

He pinned up his last button to his flannel shirt; his hands were sweating a little bit more today, he turned on the television and immediately heard the Announcer:

"Today there will be a rally for the black matters movement."

"There will be a lot of people here today standing for what they think is right."

Sam made a distasteful face, turning it off. He was tired of the Black movement and wanted to stand for something that he was taught, and he wanted to speak up and stand confidently from when his grandfather talked to him about standing for what was right.

With all the riots he had seen on television through the week, he could not sit back and do nothing, he planned to go to that rally a few days before. Being that he was in the police force, he had to stand up for the blue he wore.

Sam grabbed his keys to his 2000 pickup truck and put two picket signs in the back that read: *"Blue Matters, USA!"* He made the signs the night before with Ruby.

He went back inside the house and grabbed water out of the fridge upstairs where his dad was.

"Dad I am going to the rally, make sure you do not drink all the beers at once." Sam announced. His dad was sitting in his recliner smoking a cigarette watching the hockey game.

"Yeah," going to do what your old pops did huh?" He grumbled his laugh. "It is like the 1960's all over again", he continued with a growl.

His dad had a prejudice background being from the south.

"Yeah, okay pops I will see you later," he said as he shut the door. Sam was not racist he just thought the black matters movement was exaggerated, he had no understanding.

* * *

Ruby, wearing a pink hoodie and jeans rung the bell to his apartment.

"Hey baby," he said as he opened the door, he looked deep into her deep blue eyes as he ran his fingers through her natural blonde hair and kissed her.

Her family were southern royalty, and her family's history went back.

"You are going to that rally with me?" Sam asked grabbing his jacket.

"I guess, but I don't see the point, I am tired of this black-white feud," Ruby said flipping her hair.

"Well just think of it as a date, if you do not want to go with me, you do not support the cops that save our lives." He reminded her.

Ruby got in the truck as Sam opened the door for her, then he started it and put on the radio which rang out their favorite country song.

"I cannot believe we are going to do this," Ruby said as she was scared as to what could happen.

As they pulled up, there were many people of different color protesting.

Sam parked outside the barricades on a side street. They picked up their signs and joined the blue side of the rally.

"Blue Matters." They chanted.

"Black Matters!" One yelled close to Sam's face.

"You have no idea what we have been through or our ancestors!" One black matters protestor screamed out.

"Get over it!" Ruby yelled.

"It happened so many years ago!" Shouted Sam.

They raised their picket signs higher while chanting louder. As it turned to night, it was starting to get overcrowded.

There were so many people; some were getting into fights as the police started to lose control of the crowd, Sam lost Ruby as everyone started to be combined.

"Ruby!" he yelled out.

Sam turned around to see where Ruby disappeared to. She was nowhere in sight. It went dark.

When Sam blinked it surprised him because this woman was dark in complexion but had captivating eyes and her body fit in her outfit naturally, her hair was coiled, and she was wearing black and blue nail polish, her sign read, "Peace."

Sam could not look away from her he was stuck on her beauty, he stopped seeing color she helped him up off the ground, Sam was staring.

"I am Rein," She said as she held out her hand. Confused, Sam shook her hand.

"What's your name," Rein asked.

"I am Sam," he said focused on her beautiful dark brown skin as the shadows of light reflected off her.

At this point they were both mesmerized by each other's presence.

"Babe!" Ruby found her way back to him and grabbed his shoulders back into the real.

"Baby we should go," Ruby whined. It broke his concentration on this woman's view.

"Bye, he said,

"I will see you around Sam, Rein said.

"Who was that babe" Ruby's voice shouted over the crowd,

"That was the most beautiful woman I have ever seen," Sam said in his head.

"Who was that Sam? Ruby's voice was angered and agitated.

"It was just a protestor, Ruby." Sam said confidently.

Ruby and Sam found their way out of the large crowd. They walked to where the truck was parked which was spray painted "Evil" on the passenger door. Sam kicked the wheel.

"We should have just stayed home got take out and watched a movie," exhaled Ruby.

With a smile, Sam said quietly "I am glad we came." He would not have stumbled on elegance, Rein.

Finding Rein

Chapter 2

"Let's just go home," Ruby at this point was complaining that she had work later that night and needed sleep. They got in the truck and drove back to Sam's apartment. Sam ran straight to the bathroom

"Babe what's the rush? Ruby said clicking through channels as she plopped on the sofa.

"I got to take a piss Ruby, is that okay?"

Ruby looked annoyed and was upset at him for dragging her out there to that dangerous place.

Sam's thoughts retorted back to the woman he saw at the rally; her face being slightly rounded her hair was curly but dense she had no makeup on except for red lip gloss. With the silhouette of her shape, he could only imagine what he could do to her.

He splashed his face with cold water staring at himself in the mirror while images of

Rein's smile popped up in his head, he grabbed the towel and wiped it quickly.

He walked out and saw Ruby watching television on his flat screen. Her complexion was pale; she had a great body and the sexiest legs.

She saw him staring at her, she lit up and walked towards him as she stripped down to her red laced thong biting her lip creeping closer to him.

"Is this what you like?"

Sam was thrown on the bed as she climbed on top of him.

"You smell so good, Ruby whispered in his ear, He quickly took his shirt off as Ruby rubbed her fingers up and down his chiseled body. His rugged red short beard rubbed up against her cheek as he grabbed the back of her neck softly and kissed her soft pink lips. He touched her delicate breasts and body, as the steam of passion rolled off their bodies, touching each other's fleshy parts gripping, shaking.

Her seductiveness made him attached to her sexually with his emotions disconnected. He held her close as they felt each other let go.

"Oh Sam!" she cried out dipped in ecstasy. Their relationship was not going to last long, Sam knew what he wanted, and it was not Ruby.

She had fallen asleep with the covers between her legs with a piece of hair over her eye it was perfect, she was the same color as him — the same.

He kept replaying Rein in his mind craving her. "Rein," he said in a quieter voice. He got up and slipped his boxers back on. As he sat on the edge of the bed, he blanked out thinking about her with her magnetizing eyes, and he could not get his mind off her. He put the rest of his clothes on and woke Ruby up to get ready for her shift at the bar that night, as his thought drifted away.

In the morning.......

Sam walked into the big luxurious kitchen in his dad's section of the house and grabbed some chicken salad he made the day before.

"So, you and this girl Ruby, is a thing?" asked his dad as he walked into his kitchen with his beer belly touching the counter, as he reached for a plate.

"I mean we are a thing, yeah I guess," Sam replied.

"Son you either are, or you are not,

Your twenty-seven and have a career your set for life son, and Ruby looks like she is the one for you."

His dad would disown him dating black women, but he did not care, somehow, he was going to find Rein again.

"Listen, dad, who I date is none of your business really, and Ruby is not the one." Sam added.

Sam sensed a peace in Rein. He wanted that as a wife; to settle down with, have babies, he was getting ahead of himself he thought.

Worried about what his father would say if he found out, he planned to break it off with Ruby and give her some excuse as to why he could not be with her anymore and slowly Sam would introduce his dad to Rein.

It was starting to get complicated; he thought what if he got in contact with "Rein," he must have said her name so many times in his head. He was going to try, so what if his dad did not like it, he found her to be profound. He needed a woman like that.

Sam wanted to investigate her body, her breast, her mind. He had to find her and ask if she wanted to go on a date with him. Another rally was going to happen the following week, and he was going to be there to soften her heart and do something he never thought of in his life to do. He was going to step out of his comfort zone.

* * *

Rein walked up the stairs to her apartment and greeted her dog.

"I met a man at the rally," she said looking at paws while picking him up.

"I might have fallen in love."

"His lips looked soft, he had the best abs, and I could tell because he was wearing a tight but snug jacket."

"Guess what he was on the blue matters side aren't we just lucky that I am attracted to a person who does not like black women." Rein said.

Paws stared at her and started to look at her sideways...

"Yeah, I know you do not understand." Rein said petting Paws.

"He had the sexiest dimples." Rein continued as she put paws down.

Rein knew he was feeling her because of the way he stared at her. Her legs were trying not to go weak. Rein had to keep it together in the middle of her living room.

Rein's taste in men was Sam's type rugged strong and white. Her eyes were almond shape, she had a full shaped pear body. Rein manipulated her hair by twisting it the night before and tied it down with her mothers' red scarf who died of brain cancer, it had taken a toll on her body, and she could not fight anymore.

Rein thought back to when her mother came to her high school graduation. Her mother was so proud of her. Rein's mother being, an immigrant and poor, she wanted Rein to have a better life then her, she was a cleaning lady but when Rein started working, she started pitching in to pay for the bills in their old apartment.

Rein had accumulated some debt from her mother's medical bills and was gradually paying them off with her working in a private practice where all the rich people went to get treated.

She was getting sick and tired working for her practice and wanted to help people who did not have insurance, people who could not afford it.

Rein only knew hard work and persistence. She did not need anyone to be there for her like her father whom she had never met.

Rein did not remember him, and she did not want to meet him now. It was too late for them to even have a relationship, she was successful and took pride in herself.

Being twenty-four she was mature for her age and knew what she wanted. She had the career, now all she needed was a family.

Rein was not going to fail in meeting Sam again she had to know who he was, a little curiosity would not kill the cat, she couldn't get his face out of her head.

She went to the bathroom and washed up brushed her teeth and went into bed.

Her 30-inch screen tv was blasting out a reality tv show where random people would call random phone numbers and blindly date that person.

Rein pulled Paws close and fell asleep wrapped up in her sinful thoughts of what she wanted to do with Sam's body. The thought of him making love to her with rose petals in the bed was her last thought of him.

The television automatically turned off.

In the morning, Rein woke up to the alarm on her phone going off. Today she thought she might have the power to quit her job, but Rein had bills she must have hit the snooze button ten times that morning because it was 8:30, she was late. Rein raced to the bathroom and didn't even put makeup on. She put deodorant under her arms while the toothbrush hung out of her mouth all while trying to take out the twist in her hair. She was afraid she was not going to catch the train.

Rein slid on her Mary Janes, fed Paws, grabbed her pocketbook as she put her jacket on and raced out the door down the stairs and out of the building. Waving a taxi down, one finally stopped,

"Where to miss?" asked the taxi driver.

"To the train station, please." Rein stated. Which was several blocks down

"Thank you," she said as she got out the taxi's side door and raced down to the subway, she heard the doors closing for her train, "All doors closing," The announcer said.

"Shit." She missed it. Rein raced back up to try to catch the bus. She looked at the flat screen for the bus schedule, _not on time_ it read. Rein was not going to try to catch another taxi or uber.

Instead she ran in to her favorite bagel shop.

As Rein opened the door to get a quick bagel with cream cheese and coffee there, he was. She got in line and was next,

"Yes, can I get a lightly toasted bagel please and a black coffee."

Sam was sitting down looking at a magazine that had motorcycles plastered all over it. She did not know what to do or how to act as she waited for the bagel. Rein saw him eyeing her. The bagel shop was busy as another person bumped into her, she put her hands out to stop her from falling and was caught by him, this perfect looking man.

Sam picked her up a little.

"Umm, Rein?" He said

Sam looked surprised to see her in his bagel shop that he always came to in the morning before he went to work. "Sam, right?" Rein asked.

She looked deep into his eyes as she regained her balance and shook her stare off his glance.

"Yes," Sam said, as he hid his glee.

"Will you sit with me," he motioned.

She hesitated but sat with her bagel and tried not to stare too hard at his handsome, masculine face.

Rein felt herself looking at his neck and then lips, nose, his green eyes she could not contain herself as she blurted out,

"I have to go; I'm so late." Rein said

"Wait, where are you going?" Sam said getting up quickly almost knocking his coffee to the ground.

"I am going to be late for work." She said walking towards the door with coffee and bagel in hand.

Sam knew he had to stop her. When was he going to have a chance like this again?

"I'll take you." Sam motioned.

"That is okay," Rein shyly said.

"No, I will not let a beautiful woman like you walk," He continued

"Are you sure?" What was she doing, he was a stranger? Rein thought.

However, she could not stay away from his essence his cologne smelt so masculine. A thought came to her of undressing him with her eyes.

"Okay, Rein said looking back at him exiting the bagel store.

"Just don't kidnap me." She added.
They both left and got into his pickup truck.
She was nervous but didn't know how to talk in front of him he was doing all the talking, and she did not hear a word he was saying.

"So where do you work? He glanced shortly at her.

"Its 50 blocks from here but you can drop me off before you get to it. Rein said taking another sip and bite of her bagel.

"Rein, it's okay, I will drop you directly in front of your job." Sam said

He sounded like a person who took control, rough around the edges type.

"Okay well, it is straight up I will tell you where it is." Rein said

"So what is it that you do?" Sam asked thinking of kissing her lips.

His smile was gorgeous as she side eyed him.

"Well I help people, it is a routine thing." Rein joked.

"So that means you are a mechanic?" "A bull rider?" Sam joked with her.

Her smile made Sam more inquisitive his problems seemed to disappear forgetting about Ruby, he was stuck to her, her teeth were perfect white, she smelled like sunflowers soaking up the sun.

"Oh, right here!" Rein blurted out.

He came to a halt and ran to open the door for her.

"Ahh! Sam said, As he looked at the building sign, he read,

"Lohman's Specialist Centre"

"A doctor?" "A Nurse?"

"Yes, I am a doctor." Rein said as she walked up to her job.

"Thank you," Sam, as she looked back with wanting to kiss his luscious lips Rein walked in and headed to the desk to sign in.

She felt from that night at the rally he was going to be an interesting man. Sam turned around trying not to lose control then he remembered he did not know when he would meet Rein again, he ran inside the clinic.

"Hey Rein," he pulled her aside, is it too much to ask for your number? Rein gave a daunting look.

"How about I take your number," Rein said courageously.

"Okay," Sam sounded excited with a sexy, mysterious demeanor, he slipped his number in her hand and held her hand letting go ever so slightly not wanting to let go. Reins knees wanted to buckle, but she held herself together and tried to walk away without screaming for joy. Sam was all hers.

A Date

Chapter 3 ·

The Next Day.......

Rein texted Sam, as she picked up, she wrote:

Rein: Hey, texting you, so you have my number.

Sam: I had a dream about you. (Why did he text that he thought, couldn't take it back now.)

Rein: Yeah. what was the dream about? (Hmm already dreaming about me. Rein thought.)

Sam: Can I come see you and tell you about it.

Rein pressed Sam's number, and it dialed, three rings

Then a deep voice rang over the phone.

"Hello?"

His voice was so sexy and thick it gave her good chills.

"What do you mean to come over?" Rein was not sure.

"Well, I do not usually do that." Rein said to Sam in a Sassy but sexy voice.

Sam was not going to push it.

"Okay, what about dinner?" Sam asked.

She walked around her bedroom twirling around like a girl in love,

"Where are you taking me?" Rein said as she closed her eyes, she was wrapped in bliss.

"Well, I guess you will have to see when I get your address to come to pick you up." Sam said

Rein smiled,

"I heard you smile," Sam said slyly.

"No, you did not" she turned in a circle almost falling to the ground.

"Okay, I'll text my address." Rein said hanging the phone up

She had given in.

I will be there to pick you up at 6:30 pm" Sam texted.

He could not wait to see how the night was going to play out. He got ready.

Rein anticipated him coming to the door and scooping her up in his tanned, muscular hands and making love to her right on her fluffily rug. Tossing and turning with him (oh Sam) ... his hair smelled like hazelnuts. His hands gripping her body just imagining his body on top of hers made her want to.... The doorbell rang,

"Who is it?" She walked towards the door. "It is Sam did you forgot I was coming?"

"No, didn't think you would be here this soon."

Rein was now regretting giving Sam her address and was not ready for him to come into her space. She had some type of feelings for Sam but didn't want to be evident about them.

"Are you going to make me stand out here all-day?" Sam's deep voice echoed through the door It seemed to hit her through her body because as soon as he had said that she gave in and let him in.

Rein was wearing a blue dress with black trim at the bottom with her chocolate legs flowing so effortlessly into the background of her essence. She looked heavenly.

He did not know what it was about her that made him attracted to her. She smelt like honey and lavender which gave him a spell that made Sam want to lay with her in bed all day and talk and treat her like she was supposed to be treated.

Rein walked over as he handed her tulips.

She was taking the risk of letting Sam in her apartment, she barely knew him.

"So, can we go on that date now?" he asked.

"Yeah, I am ready to go." Rein replied

So, what are you thinking?   Sam said opening the door for her then got in the truck racing to open the door to hear her answer?

"Well, I am not sure." Rein replied.

"What did you have planned"? She said nervously, but when she was around Sam, she felt this love surrounding her.

"Well I planned something, but I cannot tell you." Sam said with one hand on the steering wheel.

They pulled up to a parking lot where there were a bunch of cars staring at a white big movie screen.

"Sam?" "How did you even find this place.?" Rein sounded surprised.

"Well I looked up an app, and it gave me this location, Sam said reaching back for a picnic basket that was collapsible.

"You cooked also?" Rein asked.

Sam had her at a drive-in movie. This man was going all out for her, but why? Rein could not wrap her mind around it.

"So, I made some basic picnic stuff," He said looking into her eyes wallowing in the thought of grabbing her close and kissing her on her soft cupid's bow.

Rein had smelled so good it was overwhelming it flowed through the truck and surrounded his nostrils with flare.

The movie was about to start, the parking lot got dark, and everyone got quiet except for the sounds of lovemaking in a tinted Escalade, that was parked three cars down from them.

Sam and Rein laughed and continued to watch and eat their late-night picnic dinner.

* * *

"That was a good movie." Rein said as Sam drove back to her place.

"The part where he got on his knee and a duck came flying in, hilarious." She snorted a little.

"Did you just snort?" Sam said, genuinely smiling at her.

She was perfect, Sam thought.

They left the parking lot and started to drive back, Sam suddenly saw flashing lights behind him and pulled over.

"Move over," the cop blurted through the megaphone. Sam stopped on the side and let the police go.

Rein was holding onto the dashboard in a panic; fear had struck her as she maintained her breathing.

"Um, are you okay?" Sam asked with the car still in park.

"I am fine." She replied but stayed quiet the rest of the ride home.

"Hey, I had a great night tonight," Sam said as he pulled up to her complex and parked the car.

"Me too," Rein replied.

"Are you sure you are okay?" Sam said, looking at her intensely.

Rein looked down as tears started to fall.

"Sam back there when the police flashed his lights, I got a little nervous, I was once stopped the first time in high school, he did inappropriate things to me, there was no one there to help me, I went to my graduation and gave my speech that day.

Rein could not believe she blurted out the words that were coming out her mouth.

Sam sat quietly and couldn't say anything. He did not know Rein well, but he would be her protector so that she would not get hurt again.

He grabbed Rein and hugged her before she got out of the truck and entered her apartment building.

"Thank you for the date, and I am sorry about the crying thing."

"It's okay Sam said. What else could he say since he was a police officer himself. How would that make him look to Rein? He thought.

He made it a priority to call her as soon as he got home and make sure she was okay.

He drove home re-thinking about what he stood for after Rein told him her life experience with the police officer that raped her.

The Second Date

Chapter 4

At his apartment where his off-girlfriend Ruby met him, he did not know how to tell her that he wanted to break it off. It was now or never.

"Ruby listen we are not working out anymore." "Can we just be friends?" Ruby chuckled a little and pushed her way in through the door to the couch and sat down.

"Sam are you serious?" Ruby said, she was strong, but Sam was her world.

"I just don't want to be in a relationship right now; Sam said looking away."

"Is there another bitch?" Sam? She was starting to sniffle, her eyes and cheeks started turning red.

Finally, Ruby let out a shriek then cry.

"Ruby I just don't think I am ready for this type of relationship."

Ruby turned to face Sam.

"I thought we were ready for the next step in our relationship? Ruby cried, with a broken heart. She was tight, dense, desolate. Ruby got up and walked out his door.

"If I walk out your door you will never be able to get me back; there is no turning back." Rub said looking at him while opening the door.

"I am sorry Ruby," Sam said.

"Yeah, you are making a big mistake Sam." Ruby said slamming the door. She started her car and drove away. He was ready to face his dad's judgment. Besides, it was his life, Sam wanted Rein.

The next morning, the weather cascaded rain drops and lightning storms that looked like a monsoon. There were big lakes everywhere. Sam drove through them like they were puddles, as he drove faster, attempting to get to Rein before she left for the morning to go to work. Luckily, he had off work and texted Rein to wait for him.

Rein was standing outside with a black umbrella over her head. Sam quickly got out and opened the door for her.

"Good morning, Sam, she cutely looked at him, while staring with full cheeks and cultivating eyes.

"Thank you very much for picking me up I cannot wait until my car is out of the shop," Rein continued.

"Rein, I chose to pick you up it is not a problem," Sam re-assured her.

She was dressed in a skirt that showed her dark brown erogenous legs.

"Can we go on another date?" Sam looked at her as they were stopped at a stop light.

"I.... Rein said.

"Wait before you answer I have this perfect restaurant you have to try. Sam interrupted.

"I... I... would love to." Rein had given in again. He was so handsome and daring, Rein thought.

"I cannot wait for tonight" Sam said as he held the umbrella over the truck door for her walking her to her job's front door.

"You are such a gentleman." "What are you hiding?" Rein said as they both walked to the door with the rain turning into a drizzle.

"Nothing," Sam said convincingly.

He wanted to let her know so bad and reveal to her the secret he was holding but was scared as to what actions would cause them not to date.

"Okay, Rein said and took the umbrella leaving him in the light rain. She went inside.

"Hmm second time in a row huh?" One of her nurses said carrying a chart looking her up and down.

"Leigh shut up," Rein said

"He looked hot in the rain." Leigh continued to tease her.

Rein threw a cotton ball at her.

"Hi, Mr., Mang what brings you in today?" She asked as she walked into a patient's room.

* * *

Sam stopped at the flower shop to get her blue and white roses. His thoughts drifted as he walked towards the limo he rented for their night, he was going all out for Rein. The night was clear, and all the stars were out.

"Stop right here," he directed the driver. Sam rung her apartment bell.

"I will be right down," Rein said with verve in her tone through the speakers.

Rein had picked out a black dress that was fitted to her frame.

She had flat ironed her hair which was down her back; her lips were a tint of blue which was her favorite color. Reins make up was light and natural. The blue bottoms stilettos finished her outfit. She grabbed her clutch and locked her apartment door.

She walked down the stairs as she texted her best friend, Charlie.

Rein: "I am going on another date.

Charlie: Again, what do you see in this dude did you guys have sex yet?

Rein: He is romantic and very friendly and no we did not have sex.

Rein put her phone away as other messages vibrated her purse.

She walked out the front door to be greeted by Sam and the limo.

"All this for me?" Rein blushed,

Sam walked towards her. He wanted to take her back to her apartment and treat her to some ooh and ahhs as he looked at her figure getting into the limo.

He rubbed his freshly cut beard as he handed her the roses.

"You look so beautiful. Sam said.

He was glued to Rein's magnificent face, hair. Sam wanted to pull it so bad. Rein got in the limo, then Sam.

"I did not expect this," Rein said looking at Sam.

"I wanted to make this night special for you, I want to spoil you," Sam continued as he looked at her, Sam got close and whispered in her ear,

Mm, I just want to take that dress off you."

Rein was taken aback and pushed his chest back softly.

"No, I am not ready to do that yet." Rein said seriously.

Sam wanted to feel her rich cakes and kiss her ample full colorful lips. He moved in to catch her off guard. She put her hands on his chest once again. No means no Sam, Rein gently smiled.

He was not given up; they stopped at the fancy restaurant Locust, it had a bistro where couples fancied in each other's company making adorations to their conversations.

"This place is beautiful Rein whispered to Sam holding his hand while walking inside towards the host.

"Good evening Sam said, he was wearing a nice suit and black shoes. The restaurant was exclusive.

"Follow me," the host said.

"Oh, you come here often?" Rein said to Sam.

"Well, I have been here on several occasions to see the building manager." Sam said.

"I'll shut my mouth now," Rein said with a grin."

"No please keep talking, Sam said as they sat down in their private area.

"Can I start you out with some wine?" The waiter asked.

"Yes please, can we have the Sweet Red wine," Sam asked while he looked at Rein.

"Yes sir, I'll be right back."

"This is such a nice place Sam, It is so fancy," Rein said as she looked around. She had not been to a fancy restaurant in her life. It was always bodegas or fast food.

"I remember when this lot was a bunch of abandoned buildings, they built it up nicely," Sam said.

The waiter came with their wine.

"Thank you," they both said in unison then laughed.

"You are so amazing." Sam said looking at her hypnotizing eyes.

"Thank you" she replied.

"Let's get to know each other," Sam was reaching for her hand.

"But after we order," Rein interrupted taking her hand away. The lust for Sam was too high even to let him touch her hands.

Something about him made her feel like she was wanted.

"Are you ready to order. The waiter asked.

"Yes, we are," answered Rein clearing her throat.

"I will have the potatoes and the salmon with lemon pepper seasoning no substitutions, just tell the chef to surprise me."

"Yes, Mam." The waiter looked at Sam.

"I'll have what she is having, I will try the same thing." Sam said.

"Oh, so you are a copycat now." Rein stared him down with a sexy smirk.

She was playing hard to get with him; she wondered if he noticed.

An excellent jazz band was playing, which had Rein's attention.

Sam got up and walked over to Rein as the lights started to dim.

"Will you dance with me?" he asked

"Did you plan this?" Rein said blushing

"Maybe," Sam said as he put out his hand out to hers.

She grabbed it and stood up as he whisked her away, floating on air.

He was so close to her.

He grabbed her back and held her tightly not letting go as they danced until their food came.

"This is how I wanted everything to be, Rein whispered in Sam's ear.

"You can have more than this," he whispered back in her ear.

"Well on that note lets go eat our food," Rein said.

They both went and sat down to eat after the song was finished.

"So where are you from?" Sam asked

"Well I am from Brooklyn but, My mom was from Africa, and my dad who is not in my life is American, My mom died a few years back when I was in high school of Cancer." Rein said putting a slender piece of fish in her mouth.

"What about you?" Rein asked as she ate her Salmon.

"I am American I grew up in South Carolina then moved to New York after I graduated high school. My mom also died of Cancer when we moved here." Sam said in a sad tone.

Rein related to that type of pain.

"Was your mother as beautiful as you were?" Sam asked. Rein blushed.

"Nice pickup line," she joked.

Rein ate her last bite.

"Would you like dessert?" the waiter asked.

"No thank you." Rein said to the waiter.

"Sir?

"No thanks," Sam said as he paid the bill.

They made their way to the limo.

They met each other's faces as Rein got closer to his face.

Rein kissed him quick, "sorry it was the wine." She said embarrassed to feel his soft lips on hers.

Sam was surprised she had kissed him.

"Rein you should not have done that." Sam said.

"I wanted to; I had a great time with you." Rein said getting closer to his face again but Rein kissed him a little bit longer. He was satisfied and wanted more. Rein laughed and bit her lip.

"I get what I want, and at the end of the night, I will have you screaming my name," Sam said, close to her neck sending chills down her spine.

The limo was on the highway on the way to the next location that he set up.

"This is a surprise so close your eyes so that I can put this blindfold over you." Sam said.

"You are not going to kidnap me, are you?" Rein said with blind fold on.

"No, you are going to love this." Sam looked out the window.

She felt the limo stop. He guided her out and led her to the dock where there was a yacht with rose petals that led onto the boat. He took the blindfold off.

Rein gasped as she put her hands to her mouth, "this is beautiful, she replied.

"It is not done yet." Sam took her face and kissed her passionately pulling her close grabbing her assets as fireworks went off over the harbor.

Rein side eyed the view of the fireworks; she stopped him.

"Fireworks? Seriously?"

She grabbed him and kissed him as she dragged him below. At this point, she was drunk from the wine she had at the restaurant.

"Wait, wait,"

Sam said this is not my boat I just rented it."

"Really? "Well, I still want you so are we still going to do it or what?" Rein coaxed.

Sam loved her edginess while she was drunk.

She grabbed his tie and kissed him more.

"Listen, Rein, I want you so bad, but maybe we should wait until another time," Sam said unsure.

"Let's go! Rein announced.

She was tipsy, and Sam knew he had to get some water in her and get her home to bed.

"We are going to go home now Rein," Sam said guiding her into the car.

"I am not drunk Sam I want you all over me this is how I feel, I want you just to do it all night." Rein said stumbling over pebbles walking to the car.

"That is all you want though right; you do not want a real relationship with me? Sam asked her.

"You are the perfect guy Sam but not for me, I like you and want to be involved, but I am scared that my heart will be broken."

She passed out.

She did have a point Sam thought, but he wanted something more with Rein. He wanted to be with her for the rest of his life he knew he found his soul mate even though she was currently passed out on his leg, it did not matter.

He tried to sober her up by giving her water. She came around a little before he dropped her off and walked her up to her apartment. He took her shoes and zipped down her dress. The rhythm in her back had him standing at attention it was perfect, and he had to leave before he did something that he would regret.

Protect

Chapter 5

Her head was bumping something serious that morning.

"Shit," she groaned, "what the hell happened last night..." She remembered last night that she had to much wine and shots; she was in her pajamas.

"Did Sam put me in Pajamas...." She thought.

She sent him a text.

Rein: Hey did you get me dressed last night?

Sam: Yes, I did not touch anything I just couldn't leave you in your dress.

Rein: I had a great time last night.

Sam: Me too, when would you like to do it again?

Rein: After I passed out and embarrassed myself? I do not know.

Sam: You were not that bad you did want to take me for yourself though.

Rein stopped texting him for a moment.

Sam: Hello?

Rein: Yeah, I am sorry about last night I am, and if I said anything crazy, I did not mean it.

Rein: I am sorry I was forward towards the end of the night.

Sam: It's okay I liked those beautiful full lips you kissed me with, we will get together this weekend I have to take you somewhere.

Rein: Well this time I will not drink as much.

She went to her best friend Charlie's contact.

Rein called her best friend, Charlie. The phone picked up.

"Hey girl what's up?"

"Hey girl!"

Charlie was a model, black and Korean were in her makeup. She had a skinny frame and beautiful straight hair; she had a one-year-old girl.

"Can you video chat?"

"Not right now babe I am at a shoot, I will call you a little later, I am sorry."

"It's okay I just wanted to talk about my date last night with...."

There was a click before she could finish the sentence. She must have been busy to just hang up like that.

They met back in college while Rein was studying medicine and while Charlie was studying men and sorority life.

They had met in the line of the vegetarian cafeteria and were both vegetarians at the time and were exploring their new-found diet which made them decide to become vegetarian friends. The relationship grew to go out to the mall or going to concerts to see their favorite R&B singers. There wasn't a single moment that Charlie was not there for her best friend and Rein was always there for her.

Rein went to the kitchen to fix some food. She enjoyed making her apple salads mixed with blue cheese. She picked up the phone and called Sam her love story

Hello?

"Hey, beautiful? Sam's deep voice rang over the phone, "what are you doing?"

"I am just sitting here watching this reality show." Rein said.

"This may be a little out of the ordinary, but can I come over?"

Rein paused, she did not want to get in trouble and slip on his Johnson, she was not ready for that, or was she.

Rein was going to take a chance,

"Yeah, you can bring some ice cream over and popcorn. Rein said anticipating his warm touch on her.

"Okay Rein, I will see you soon." Sam said.

Rein went to get cleaned up. She dressed in some sweats and a sweatshirt. There was a knock on the door. Coming she said, he was here early she thought. She opened the door not thinking to look through the peephole.

In rushed a man who was tall and masculine, Rein leaped back as the man came towards her looking savage ready to attack her.

"What are you doing here?

"I am going to give you something that you will never forget."

He was white and had a bald head with a medium build,

"You want to go be with white men let me show you how a real white man gets it done."

Rein broke down into her cat stance which is a form of Ninjutsu, don't even come near me right now, just as she was about to kick him, Sam walked in, in his amazement he notices the man's face it was his friend who wasn't too fond of different races, him and Sam grew up with each other.

Sam grabbed him before he could touch Rein.

"What the hell Larry what are you doing here he pulled him out into the hallway,"

Rein at this point was confused,

"Give me one minute, Rein," as he closed the door.

"How the hell did you find this place?" As Sam held his collar.

"I followed you, your ex told me to keep tabs on you, and now I see why you dumped her ...to go out with this nig... Larry stopped short. "Whoa!" Sam yelled

"Get out of here and don't come back here!" Sam said dusting off his shirt.

"You can tell her whatever the hell you want." Sam continued yelling at Larry as he ran away.

"All right man but don't come running when your old man kicks you out of the house." Larry yelled back with a grin. Shit was about to hit the fan.

"Am I supposed to pretend that did not just happen?" Rein said walking up to Sam as he held his head bent.
"What am I supposed to do if my dad finds out?" Sam said worried.

"Sam if you do not want to be with me just say it." Rein said folding her arms.

"Rein you are the most beautiful girl I have ever met I do not ever want to give up on you; I fell in love ever since the rally and I have changed." Sam said realizing he was falling for Rein.

"Sam what if your dad does kick you out?" Rein said.

"Let him I can just find another place to live, I have backed up assets." Sam said coming closer to Rein.

Rein looked at him focusing on his lips and went in for a kiss.

He pulled her close with his hand on her lower back where her dimple met which connected with her cake. He could feel the imprint which made him want to rip off her clothes. Rein pushed him away gently.

"I cannot, you know if we get involved there is no going back right," Rein said with her hands on his polished build.

Sam looked at her,

"I am in for the long, brutal haul of judgment and want you to meet my family, as crazy as that sounds." He said walking over to the couch. They sat down.

"We will work it out." Sam said as Rein relaxed her hands as he pulled her closer to watch the movie. Their relationship and bond were starting to come together.

Duty Calls

Chapter 5 1/2:

"What's your 10-20." Sam's intercom blasted through the radio.

"I have arrived at the scene."

"I will meet you there." The other voice rang over the intercom.

Crowds started to gather around as Sam stood with his gun in his holster. Another man dead by gang violence. He could see the crowd getting more significant with their phone's recording the scene. One man stepped to close to the body.

"Sir, please have some respect, step back," Sam said.

More police cars showed up.

"Well, he did not even have time to get to the fence," a detective said in the background,

"That went right through his head," a rookie blurted out.

"Montgomery before you leave, I need a statement."

Sam walked up to the detective and gave his statement.

"As I was running for the perp, I heard gunfire on the east end, as I got there another man ran off he was a black male with a medium build gang color on his pants."

"All right Montgomery thank you for the statement."

"No problem," Sam replied looking out to the crowd as he tried to control them to disperse as the coroner put the body in their van.

* * *

Rein had just finished her last patient for the day; she texted Sam;

"Hey, where are you?" weren't you supposed to meet me today?"

She clicked the phone off the main screen and continued to grab her things and walked out the door.

"Hey! He yelled as he pulled up next to her, Sorry I am late he said as he revved the engine.

"Sam it's no problem," she said looking at him with complete fullness in her voice. Sam didn't tell her yet that he was a police officer.

"So how was your night?" Sam asked as he drove with one hand on the wheel with starry eyes while searching Rein's eyes for the answer.

"Well, it started with this patient having pains in his abdomen I had to check his stomach found out it was only gas."

Sam laughed so hard the truck swerved a little.

"Hey, you try dealing with a patient that is in so much pain, he has to come to the doctor to just pass gas."

He stopped and got out of the truck to open the door.

"Hey, Sam!" He turned around and just as he did, he was socked in the face with one blow he stumbled a little to see who punched him. Rein started to scream and went to Sam's side as they ran away.

He got up slowly as Rein lent her shoulder.

"That came out of nowhere." Sam said

"You think, let me fix your eye up," Rein said as she helped him up the stairs.

"Those guys are going to be in deep shit if I see them around here again." Sam continued to talk as blood dripped down the side of his mouth.

"Okay killer slow down," as she sat him down on the chair and got the first aid kit.

"I want you to know I am sorry for those guys knowing where you live, and if you need me, I will be here.

"I know how to defend myself if they were to come into my house." Rein said dabbing under his eye with the cotton ball.

He pulled her close, so his face was nestled in her stomach.

She was still holding the peroxide in one hand and the cotton ball in another.

As she set them down, Sam made his move as he lifted her shirt, making soft, delicate kisses on her stomach, he guided his hands up the sides of her curved back and stood up. He grabbed her body close, kissing her neck as she put her head back in ecstasy. The table was going to be their platform. He undressed her as he kissed everywhere making sure he was not hurting her.

"Sam, she whispered do you want to go to the bedroom, and do you have condoms?"

Damn it he knew he should have brought some with him; now he was stuck with his print all exposed.

"Sam, we have to stop." Rein said

She got off the table and put her shirt back on.

"Listen I will be right back!" as he scrambled for his pants and shirt and got his keys, he was going to the drug store to purchase some sex gloves.

He could not wait to make love to her.

He pulled up to the convince store on the corner and parked the car, leaving it running. Sam went down the aisle with the lube and picked up a box of condoms and walked towards the register.

At the same time in walked a man with a bandana over his face with a gun pointed to the clerk.

Sam immediately saw what was going down and took his gun out of his holster. He sneaked around the corner of the aisles and drew his gun.

Freeze! Don't move! The man dropped everything and ran out the door Sam ran after him tackling him down to the pavement.

The police showed up, "Good work Montgomery," one officer said, this guy has been hitting up every convenience store on this block."

"I was just at the right place at the right time," Sam said walking away and getting into his truck.

He was recorded chasing the man down the block, and a video of his truck had been posted to social media. He wondered if Rein would see it, he was not ready to explain what had happened and why he had a gun in the first place. He had to tell her at some point

Sam reached her apartment; He could not wait until he saw Rein so that he could make non-stop love all night.

He looked at his phone as he walked up the stairs then went to her apartment door.

Rein opened the door and looked up at him with her phone in her hands.

Sam stopped and looked at her, "I can explain,"

"Explain that you took this guy down, she exclaimed kissing him as she pulled him in.

Social media is quick that happened like 20 minutes ago. Sam thought. She had not found out his secret, and he was in the clear.

Sam thought she was going to slam the door in his face. Instead, she jumped on him.

Her thighs shivered as he grabbed her body and kissed her lumps close to her wet spot. She shrieked a little and let go.

"Sam!' she screamed as he pleasured her leaving her body numb. "It so hot," Rein muttered turning the air on.

They rolled in the sheets all night.

He went at it again. Her soft skin was undeniably supple against his. He wanted to hold her and not let her go. He slowly went down kissing her fleshy parts. They finished on the floor and slept there until morning. Sam was still asleep in the bed as Rein cooked breakfast.

"Breakfast is served," Rein said as she brought the platter to him, then went to get hers. They both sat in the bed and talked about everything they ever dreamed of.

This was the woman he wanted for the rest of his life. How did she grab hold of his mind and soul like that? She was amazing. Not to mention the effort she gave when she was on top, she was in control, and he loved that attitude in a woman.

He was going to try to make his family love her, and if it did not work, he would have to disown them.

Rein was now everything to him and of course her little dog Paws.

Five Feet Under

Chapter 6

The first few weeks with Rein was unforgettable. Sam took off for a week, so they could go out on little excursions to get away from the city life. The Pocono's wasn't that far, and so they decided to go for that week. They had to cut it short because Sam's partner died on the shift he was supposed to be doing that week.

"Rein I am sorry I have to go." Sam said

"But I thought you took off of your security job?" Sam looked back at her spread out on the bed in a delicate black lace one piece.

"So, tempting, but I need to go, I will be back, we have the rest of the week."

He felt horrible lying to her about what he did for a living; he knew if she found out she would be heartbroken.

Rein rolled her eyes as he walked over to give her a long, breathless kiss,

"I'll be back I promise." Sam said leaving.

He picked up the keys and left. Damn his partner was like a best friend, he did not blame himself for his death, but he had to be there because his father was going to be there also since he knew his family.

Sam knew a whole lot of questions were going to rise. He sped towards the funeral. He pulled up just as his father was walking up.

"Where have you been for the week?" his father stopped him. "No calls, nothing, plus that girl keeps asking me where you were; I like her."

Sam knew his father did not know he was dating a black girl, why didn't Ruby tell him, and from the corner of his eye he saw her waving him down.

Shit," Sam said in his mind.

"SAM?" Is that you?" Where have you been?" Ruby said waving.

"Well, staying far away from you." He mumbled.

"Listen we need to talk when the funeral is finished." Ruby said looking at him. He was not falling for her goo-goo eyes.

Ruby had sent his friends after him twice. Sam was serious about moving away from all of this, judgment day was here.

Everyone sat in the church. Sam had his uniform on in salute to his fallen partner. He walked up to his wife and kids; I'm sorry for your loss he said and shook each of their hands.

"His wife hugged Sam while whispering,
"He would not have died if he had to work your shift while you were out with your new girlfriend who seems to be not fond of your fathers taste in a woman for you, Jimmy told me everything."

Sam pulled away softly and slowly he was feeling bad he had taken off while his partner was out with a rookie, he thought a little harder about the words Jim's wife said as a tear fell from his eyes.

"I am sorry Mam," he said sitting with his precinct. His father eyed him suspiciously, and Ruby gave him a severe look, it was like the whole world was blaming him for his partner's death he had to leave. He did not have to prove anything to anyone. Sam thought.

The services ended as Sam said his goodbyes. Ruby stopped him.

"Listen, Sam, I wanted us to work, but I guess we just didn't, you like bitches with dark ass skin, and I did not tell your father yet, but you need to rethink of getting back with me before he finds out." She said folding her arms.

"Listen, Ruby, after you sent those guys to hurt me, you think I am going to run back to you?" "I do not need you or my father running my life," "Please leave me alone and I do not give a damn if you tell my father, but I am leaving."

"Also, its 2018 stop being racist." Sam finished walking away.

With that Sam got in his truck and left. He could not wait to see Rein's beautiful face and touch her glistened body to get his mind off all the drama that was starting to unfold in his life. Rein had sent a picture of her oiled-up body. He pressed harder on the accelerator forgetting he was in his police uniform.

He pulled into the parking lot, looking down he saw his uniform pin, Shit! He said to himself. He took the key out of the ignition and changed. Luckily his windows were all tinted. He put his uniform in a locked tool kit in the bed of his truck and hopped out the back locking his doors.

"Beautiful I am back," Sam said sexy.

Rein was in the bathtub soaking with a cucumber mask over her face with headphones in her ears blasting R&B.

Sam walked up to her slowly and took the earbuds out of her ears, she jolted a little then took the mask off her face and jumped hugged Sam wet and all.

"I missed you," she kissed him.

Sam had sad eyes looking at her. Is this what he wanted? He asked himself.

He had to rethink everything before it went deeper then what it already was. They spent the night making love which was terrific, but Sam wanted to leave.

"Are you ready to go home?" Sam asked Rein.

"Sam?" What's wrong?" Rein asked.

"I just want to go home I am not in the mood to be out here I will drop you home, I am sorry, Rein."

"Its fine," Rein said drying up and washing the mask off her face, putting on some clothes.

The ride was awkward going home; Rein broke the silence.

"I am sorry for the loss of your friend, and I hope you find some closure." Rein said with empathetic eyes.

"I'll give you some time, call me when you are ready." Rein continued

They arrived, and she went up to her apartment.

Sam gave her a small peck on the lips and got back into the truck and drove away.

He arrived in front of his brownstone. All his clothes were outside in a suitcase.

"Shit," he said, his father had found out and threw him out. He had to get to a bank and get his back up money. His father had lost his mind.

Sam picked up all his clothes and went into the truck just as Ruby was pulling up.

"Hey Sam, I see you got kicked out of your apartment, its mine now so if you are looking for me or want to come to hang, you know where to find me." She laughed and flipped her hair driving away.

He was about to lose it and then thought to call Rein, but he did not want to seem weak.

Sam peeled off making his way to the bank.

* * *

He took his card out as he pulled up to the ATM checking his balance, three hundred thousand dollars, he had enough to hold him over for a few months if he ate lite and cut off some memberships to the gym; the way he felt he needed a friend, Rein.

He decided to dial her number:

"Hello?" Sam said

"Hello," Rein answered in a groggy voice.

"Can we talk? I need to talk to you." The desperation in Sam's voice was urgent.

"Yeah Sam" just come over, Rein said.

"Oh yeah, I am sick by the way." She added.

"Well, I will have to work with that. Sam said hanging up.

Memories

Chapter 7:

Sam knocked on the door, there standing pretty in her pajamas Rein had tissues up her nose, and it smelled like Vicks.

"You were not joking when you said you were sick."

"I told you." Rein said locking the door behind him.

"So, what did you want to talk about?" Rein said taking the tissues out her nose.

"First off, I have to say sorry about when my friend died, and I gave you an attitude, I was just upset that I was not there for him.

"I was not mad at you." Rein sat down at the table across from him.

"What happened? You sounded upset over the phone." Rein said abated breath waiting for him to say something, so she could eagerly help him.

"My father kicked me out, and now my ex is living there she did it because I am going out with you." Sam said hitting the table fist closed. Also, my father knows I am dating you; you're the one that I am falling deeply in love with. Sam continued.

Rein stood up.

"Love with me?" Rein acted surprised.

"Yes," Rein I love you, I want you to be my girlfriend." Sam said.

Rein went over and kissed him lightly on the lips,

"I want you to be my boyfriend; Rein said looking him in his eyes trying not to get emotional and sappy.

"Look you can stay here." Rein said

"I did not want to be a problem for you." Sam looked at her.

"Sam shut up; Rein said grabbing him by his white t-shirt kissing him soulfully.

They almost forgot paws was in the room when he barked at them in agreement.

"You to paws," Sam said picking him up as a stream of pee went on his shirt.

"Oops, sometimes he does that when he gets excited. Rein said taking paws away from Sam.

"I should not have done that." Sam said taking his shirt off.

"You can wash up in the bathroom." Rein gestured to where the bathroom was.

Sam knew he was going to like it here with Rein just to be in her presence intensified everything for him; he could also work on who raped her back when she was in high school.

In Highschool...

Rein was on her way to school in her brand-new punch buggy, she always wanted one, and her mother was saving up to give it to her for her graduation. She had gotten all straight A's and was valedictorian for her class. Her mom, being raised to value education she pushed it on Rein since she was young and to love what you do and study hard to get what you want out of life.

Rein held those moments and memories of her mother. She valued the work her mother was putting in cleaning businesses every night as Rein stayed in school and studied.

One night she saw her mother passed out on the couch and covered her with a blanket. Rein continued to do that for her mother until one night she did not come home. The police had told her she was in the hospital. She had collapsed on the ground walking home and was rushed to the E.R.

Rein went to the hospital and started to pray her mother would be okay.

"Rein, her mother looked up at her with the mask on her face, I can feel myself slipping, I know I am going to die. I want you to be happy and live a successful life, find a man who loves and cherishes you, I love you so much, Rein." Her mother said taking her last breath.

With that, those were the last words that came out of her mothers' mouth.

Rein went to the funeral by herself and some of her mom's friends and co-workers, but she had no place to go which made her end up in a children's shelter for a year. Luckily, they treated her with respect since she knew how to fight. She still had her car and had to sell some things to put down on an apartment because she outgrew the children's shelter.

Her last day of high school, was when her life changed. She was running late to graduation and had to speed to get there, or she was not going to make her speech.

Police lights flashed behind her. As she pulled over to the side on a non-busy road, trees all around, she was confident enough to show the police her documents.

"License and registration please," the officer asked. Rein reached into the glove compartment and took it out of the sleeve with her License.

"Step out the car mam," he asked.

"Can I ask why?" Rein said confused as to why she had to step out.

"Mam just step out of the car and put your hands on the hood." The officer said searching her for weapons.

He started to grope Rein in places she had never been touched before. She tried to turn around and stop him, but he had a grip on her arm that she could not get out of and she was not going just to do what she learned in a dojo on a police officer.

As he was forcing himself inside her, he was sweating, squeezing her breast, it seemed to go on forever, she would never forget his moans with his grey beard touching her now tainted shoulders. It was happening, and she was frozen in time.

It went dark, cold, the pain of his penetrating tool left her thinking about nothing. She was about to graduate; her dress was ruined with bloodstained trails. She cried after he left her but found the strength to put on a black spear skirt in the trunk of her car and underwear with a black shirt. The policeman had left her there to wallow in his delight and her defeat. She saw strength even though she was in pain to get dressed and get there on time. She had no empathy to mourn the loss of her virginity at that moment.

That day Rein never told anyone, she was never comfortable with a man until Sam had wandered by her at the rally. She had forgotten about the ordeal that went on in her past. Sam made it disappear.

* * *

Sam pulled closer to Rein on the couch knowing she had something worrying her. He kissed Rein good night as they got into the bed and slept.

Sam thought back to when he graduated high school, he was well educated and went to the best schools in NY his parents paid for everything, even though he had a job mowing lawns in the suburbs of NY. He saved most of it to get his own pickup truck that wasn't too much to look at, but he fixed it up with a new coat of paint, all the girls were after him when he rolled up at school.

Sam got good grades and was always competitive in sports, especially football. He went through college without playing it and just studied law and joined the police force. His mom was always proud of him even though she was in the first stages of her cancer he had faith she would get better. He wanted her to live and took her on a cruise before she passed away.

It was her life he valued, how she raised him and taught him to love no matter what color. She carried his secrets of going out with a black girl at school in secret, so his buddies did not tease him about her race. It did not last because she moved away.

He wanted her to be his wife, but it was not in their lifetime.

When his mother passed away, his father lived life usually and had a few girlfriends. His father did not comfort him on the loss of his mother because he was a practical person... shit happens type of man. Sam knew his father was not going to like Rein. He had to ease her into the family, and hopefully, his mothers' side who lived down south would accept her.

It did not matter anymore to him though because he was stuck with Rein. They were cuddled up together as they dreamt of their memories and anxious for the next day to begin.

The Decision

Chapter 8

Rein was the whole world to him, the way he made her laugh and picked her up and kissed her. He loved the way she would get mad and turn her whole face up when she yelled.

Rein was beautiful in ways he could not explain to his family when they were going to see them in South Carolina for a family reunion the following week. Even though some of his family was racist, they would have to get used to seeing their mixed children at family events. Sam was unbothered by it, he loved Rein and intended to spend the rest of his life with her.

"Good morning beautiful," Sam said as he reached over her warm naked body to cuddle her. She was still sound asleep as he kissed her on the cheek with her hair wild and curls out. Sam leaped out of bed to prepare breakfast, Naked. He was going to put his culinary skills to the test even though he hadn't cooked a day in his life. The internet was there to help him. Sam scrambled the eggs but burnt them a little, the bacon was extra crispy and the toast, well let's say they were well done. He put everything on a plate then poured apple juice in a glass and brought it to Rein.

Rein got up with a surprised look, "for me?" "What did you do," Rein said eyeing the plate. Everything was extra crispy -burnt to a crisp.

Sam waited for her compliment.

"Wow thank you, it looks delicious. Rein said closing her eyes trying a piece of bacon as it crumbled in her mouth with a burnt taste. Then she ate the eggs with no taste.

"Sam, I love the breakfast, Thank you." Rein said continuing to eat her toast.

"Are you sure, because my cooking sucks as you can see, you want to go out and eat for breakfast. Sam said feeling sorry for putting her through that ordeal.

"I am sorry Sam, but yeah you cannot cook." Rein stated putting the plate aside on the night stand.

Taking their time to get dressed they suddenly kissed passionately.

"Don't start something we are not going to finish," Rein said staring into his eyes as they both got undressed touching each other in their secret places. Guided in each others love, they both let go of their doubts fears and pains. They wallowed in the completion of their screenplay as they went into the shower to do it again. Sam had her against the bathroom wall kissing on her neck while kissing her silhouette as he was wrapped in her longevity as he made love to Rein.

He felt her five times; he was going to marry Rein when it came time for them too. She was the one.

Rein gelled her hair into a high puff as she put makeup onto her flawless face. The clothes she was wearing made Sam want to strip them off again.

"Are you ready?" Sam asked looking at her trying to calm his oversexed emotions.

"I am ready," Rein replied.

They walked out the door.

* * *

Sam opened the door for Rein as she stepped out almost hitting her face on the pavement, he caught her with one arm, it was a cliché in a romance movie the way he caught her and looked at her kissing Rein's full lips.

"So we are going to the mall." Sam said driving.

"A favorite place for a woman," Rein said wondering what they were doing there.

"I want you to pick out something that you have always wanted, Sam said, where would you like to start?" he continued

"Well we can start at the food court where I can eat and talk to you," Rein said walking and holding his hands. He kissed her as they entered the food court area.

"I am thinking Chinese," Rein said looking at the food behind the glass.

Her mouth was watering for fried rice and barbeque spear ribs.

"I'll have some wonton soup he told the server and fried rice with Barbeque spare ribs, Two orders of that please." Sam finished.

The lady did the two orders, and Sam pulled out some cash, as he did, Ruby swiped by and took the twenty-dollar bill. Sam wanted to kick someone's ass but as he saw who it was, he calmed down.

Rein walked up to Ruby and took it back and put it in Sam's hands.

"Listen whatever you and he had is over, so you need to keep on walking and leave Sam alone, He does not deserve what you are doing to him, so back off." Rein said with a combative voice.

"Who do you think you are talking to miss black girl." Ruby said single-mindedly. Rein held her hands from throwing a punch straight to Ruby's face.

Sam broke it up before Rein could say another word.

"Hi Ruby, we were just leaving." Sam said with a quieted voice.

Ruby and her entourage walked off with smirks on their faces.

"Sam what the hell why do you let her walk all over you like that, you did not even defend me, are you sure you are here for me or am I just some black girl prize that your showing off.?"

Rein said storming off. "I'll catch the bus home." Rein yelled.

"Rein wait," He ran after her before she could walk out the mall entrance.

"Rein I want to be with you, please don't leave, if I have to, I will shout it out in this mall that I love you."

"I will do it Rein" .... He would not she thought.

"I LOVE YOU REIN." Sam shouted.

Everyone stopped and looked at him like he was crazy. Sam ran over to Rein and held her like if he was in love for the first time and gave her a long sweet, sensual kiss, they left with their food to eat at home and watch television.

The decision he had to make whether to pop the question to Rein or not was it too early? Sam

had to wait a little longer for when she met his family. The ring was a princess cut he had bought it after their second date. She was going   to   be   his   wife.

MEET THE FAMILY

Chapter 9

This was the week that Sam was not ready for. They were on their first road trip together as a couple. The family reunion they were going to in South Carolina had Sam and Rein on edge.

Sam rented a gas efficient car and drove 16 hours.

Rein did not have to drive instead she enjoyed scenery and slept. Sam pulled over in Delaware to get some snacks and use the bathroom at a rest stop.

"Babe you want anything," Sam said shaking her a little.

"Sure, just a coffee and some chips Rein said with a smile then went back to drooling a little on her car pillow.

"Sam locked the door smiling looking at his queen asleep; He hoped they liked her, they were a few more hours from his aunt's house.

Sam paid for the snacks and got in the car.

"Thank you," Rein said drinking her coffee and eating some of her chips.

"That is a weird combination Sam said looking at her disgusted.

"It is my combination, and I like it." Rein complained.

"Well, that is your decision," Sam laughed in disgust.

"Don't judge me; she said looking at him side-eyed, what combinations of food do you eat together?" Rein continued.

"Well I am not like you, I like fries and milkshakes and burgers together." Sam stated almost licking his lips.

Rein put her finger in her mouth and started to fake choke.

"What? Who does not like that combination?" Sam questioned her.

"I do not," Rein said looking out the window with a serious face.

"Sam I am a little nervous," the tone in Rein's voice was troublesome.

"Listen we are going to leave if you feel uncomfortable at any time, okay," Sam said reassuring her.

"Okay, she said looking out to the traffic that was starting to build in front of them. It was a dead standstill for 2 hours.

Sam went into the cooler in the trunk and got the sandwiches.

"What did you put in this sandwich?" asked Rein.

"It is a family secret, my mom used a combination of different spices, herbs. Sam said closing the trunk walking back to get into the driver seat.

"It's delicious!" Rein said gulping it down.

Rein was done with her sandwich by the time they were driving full speed again. They would make it by morning.

* * *

They must have pulled up to the biggest house Rein has ever seen. She looked with amazed eyes. The front of the house had two pillars holding the house up and a little garden on the side. The house wrapped around which reminded her of the white house a little.

Sam got their bags out and closed the trunk.

"This is my Aunt Hanna's house, she is not racist and prays to Buddha." Sam said.

When he lived there, she would always sneak him candies, and take care of him when his parents went on vacations.

"Oh, okay," Rein replied. How did she ever agree to this? Rein was terrified to be in another state without Charlie being aware of her whereabouts, she was taking a huge risk going into unknown territory.

The door opened wide and out came a lady dressed in all white, she had to be in her mid-50's.

"Hello, Rein!" Welcome to my home I have yawl's beds set up for you to stay for the two days. Aunt Hanna said.

She had a thick accent and was walking with pep.

Sam lifted their bags and went inside closing the house door.

"She lives here by herself whispered Rein to Sam,

"Yes, my uncle left her all this property who was my fathers' brother, Replied Sam.

"Wow," Rein said still whispering.

"So, Aunt Hanna how have you been?" Sam asked going into the kitchen where she was making snacks for them.

"I have been good, I cannot complain being eighty- five it gets lonely sometimes and having a rare disease, I'm happy to be still kickin', and I needed someone to stay with me, so your cousin Harold moved into the east side of the house.

Oh shit, Sam thought, his cousin Harold was a sheriff for the town and had been working there for years, before he could give the background of his cousin Harold Aunt Hanna continued...

"But that did not work out for him, so he moved out into town instead." Aunt Hanna said putting the sandwiches and chips in a plate for them.

"You have a beautiful home," Rein said looking around.

"Thank you, my dear, it has been a long time since this house has been here in the family, my husband left it to me, and I plan on giving it to someone when I die." Aunt Hanna said watching them with some sad tones.

Auntie, you look great for Eighty-five! Sam exclaimed to perk her feelings up.

Is this the type of charm he used on you Rein?" She asked jokingly.

"No, not really but he tries," Rein said looking at Sam in a smooth manner.

"Well let me show you where your room is.

Aunt Hanna said leading them to a beautiful master bedroom with a bath with jets in the middle of the room.

"Thank you, Aunt Hanna we are just going to rest for a little while," Sam said closing the door while she walked back downstairs.

"Wow," Rein said this room is my favorite."

"Its nice right Sam said closing the curtains taking his pants off and going over to turn on the tub.

"Take your clothes off and lock the door," Sam said seductively looking at Rein.

She locked the door and got in the tub with Sam. He held her close as her head lay on his chest while the bath filled up with warm water. She was kissing the stars right now and was feeling loved.

Rein turned around and gave him a long kiss as she climbed on top of him holding the back of his head, then looking into his eyes.

"I love you Sam Montgomery." Rein said pressing her body closer, so her breast was smashed against his chest.

"I love you too Rein Garnet." Sam said going in for a kiss. The water seemed to be getting hotter with all the love that was going through their bodies. They were in tune with each other's motions, Rein riding every way he liked, just then another door opened, and a familiar face peered in through the door.

Ruby's eyes wondered the room and her eyes got stuck on Rein and Sam making love right in the middle of the room in the bathtub.

MEET THE FAMILY

Chapter 9 1/2

"Ruby what the hell are you doing here Sam yelled getting up out the bathtub with himself exposed.

"Shit," Sam said grabbing the closest towel.

"Well, Well, what were you and her doing in your Aunts bathtub?" Said, Ruby, as she walked all the way in, giving a nasty look at Rein who was still sitting in the bath exposed. Rein gave Sam a look then got out of the tub to go to the smaller bathroom to get dressed.

"So, you bring her to the family reunion instead huh Sam." Ruby said snickering.

Sam got his clothes out of the suitcase not looking at Ruby.

"Yes, I am in love with her Ruby, and if you cannot handle it stay out of our business, You and I were nothing." Sam said putting the shirt over his head.

"Are you telling me that you do not have anything for me anymore?" Ruby asked.

"I told you I wanted you out of my life, Ruby, Sam continued.

"I am not understanding, Ruby got closer to Sam and grabbed his junk, whispering in his ear,

"We had a good thing."

Sam pushed her hands away just as Rein came out the bathroom getting dressed.

Ruby turned and walked right past Rein giving her a snooty look.

'You can have him," she said nastily, "Have fun playing cops and robbers." Ruby slammed the door walking out.

"What in the world did she mean by that?" Rein wondered, then looked at Sam he had a worried face.

"Is there something that you need to tell me?" Rein questioned.

"It's nothing, Sam said making sure she could see the happiness on his face, that it was nothing, knowing that he had to tell her before his family did or even Ruby.

Later that day, the family reunion was in a park, there were a lot of black and white couples, mixed children running around with ice cream in their hands. Sam wanted that, children from Rein. They stopped short as his father walked up to them.

"So, you are the famous Rein I have heard so much about. Sam's dad said. He held out his hand for Rein to shake it.

Sam intervened and shook his dad's hand.

His dad pulled him in close to his ear.

"What the hell you think you are doing bringing her here?" His dad said with a fake smile.

Sam pulled away but kept a smile on his face, "All right dad see you, we are going to get some food." Sam said angrily letting go of his hand.

"Nice to meet you." Rein said walking away as Sam pulled her away.

"He seems nice Rein said looking at Sam as they went towards the hamburgers.

"You do not know him very well."

Sam said looking at Rein. She was so beautiful; the sun was kissing her, he felt a little jealous.

"You are so beautiful," Sam said continueing to stare.

"Thank you, Rein kissed him and went back to, eating her burger.

Aunt Hannah had the microphone,

"Excuse me everyone welcome to the Montgomery, Ramies, and Daunty family reunion. I wanted everyone to be here; Today I would like to announce that the chief of police, my nephew Harold is retiring today. I am so proud of him and would like for him to cut this cake in remembrance of what an excellent service he did for this town and people.

Sam looked over at Rein.

"Rein are you okay Sam whispered. She was staring blankly at his cousin. Rein he whispered louder.

She snapped out of it.

"Sam, can I go sit down, I need to sit." Rein was overwhelmed because she saw a familiar face on stage and she was trying to tell herself it was not real, but he was there in life form. She wanted to tell Sam but didn't know how to.

"Sam, we need to talk, Rein pulled him off to the side, that is the man that rapped me when I was in high school.

"What?! Sam yelled some people looked back.

"What?" he whisper yelled.

"Are you sure? Sam continued. Sam did remember a time when his cousin came to visit them right around that year with his dad but his cousin was just starting the police academy.

"Shit Rein, do you want to leave." Sam said concerned.

"I do not know what to do." Rein said dying a little inside burying her face in the palm of her hands.

"Let's go; Sam said walking out of the park and getting in the rental.

By then Harold was done with his speech and caught up to them. "Where are ya will going?" Harold asked.

"Rein is not feeling too well, we are going by Aunt Hanna so that she can get some rest." Sam said thinking fast.

"All right I will see ya'll over there later." Harold turned around walking towards other family.

Rein was frozen she wanted to break down and cry but couldn't. Sam saw and held her hand as they drove back to Aunt Hanna's house.

"Rein you have to talk to me," Sam pleaded.

"I...I. cannot that can't be him. Rein wept.

She was almost rolled up in a ball in the front seat.

"This is what I am going to do for you, give you the best massage run the bath for you, lock both our room doors and you, and I can soak, no sex just talk, okay?" Sam said in a worried tone.

Rein shook her head okay. She was faced with this monster again; she should have never come. All those feelings she had for Sam were stuck at a standstill. He pulled up to the house and walked Rein upstairs.

Sam ran the bath water and gave Rein a massage which helped her to relax; Sam poured rose petals in the bath and aromatherapy soap as the bath filled up, they both sat in the warm bath, Sam holding her tight as they talked.

"Sam it was him the one that raped me, when I saw him on stage, I froze I could not believe it, he had to have recognized me right?" Rein said looking back at Sam.

"I cannot believe my cousin was the one that did this to you Rein." Sam said.

"I am not sure if he did it he just reminded me of the person that did it that is all." Rein said playing with the foam.

There was a hurriedly knock on the door. Sam got up and put a towel on to go open the door.

"It's me Aunt Hanna, are ya'll okay? You two just ran off."

"We are okay Aunt Hanna, Rein was not feeling well." Sam said with only his head out the door.

"Would you like me to get some tea, I'll make some for her, it will melt all that away." Aunt Hanna turned and walked down the half-circled stairs.

"Okay thank you, Aunt Hanna," Sam said closing the door.

Rein and Sam got dressed and strolled downstairs, to be met by his father, Ruby, Aunt Hanna and Harold sitting at the table having some left overs they had brought back.

Aunt Hanna had placed some tea next to where Rein sat down.

Sam's father looked highly upset and uncomfortable but smiled at Rein.

Ruby was happily eating her food while occasionally looking at Sam with a seductive grin.

"So, Sam what is it that you do now in New York," asked Harold.

"I am in security Sam said playing it off. Ruby went wide-eyed.

His father was quiet.

"Oh okay, and Rein what is it that you do?" Harold asked her.

Rein looked up and tried not to cower in fear, he had looked so familiar.

"I am a doctor." Rein said confidently.

Ruby mumbled something under her breath.

"What was that Ruby?" Sam asked.

"Oh nothing, I am just eating my food." Ruby said stuffing more mac and cheese in her mouth.

Sam looked down at his plate then at his father and Ruby,

"Listen both of you if you don't like Rein because of her skin color then you are no family of mine its 2018, get over it, I saw so many of our family members with other races I'm not going to stay here if you can't accept Rein being my girlfriend soon to marry fiancé."

Rein looked at him surprised. Everyone including Aunt Hanna froze.

TELLING HER THE TRUTH

Chapter 10

Rein packed her clothes while Sam stayed downstairs yelling at his father. He then met Rein in the room.

"I am sorry for the outburst with my dad, but he has to know that I love you, you are the one for me Rein." Sam said trying to get her to stay.

"I do not know what to say." Rein said picking her bags up.

"I just want to go home, only because one of your family members looks like the one that raped me years ago, can we just go, please." Rein said tired eyed.

"Yes, we can go, and we need to talk in the car about something." Sam looked at her with a serious grin.

Sam picked his bags up that Rein packed up for him she was ready to go, he wanted to be that crutch for her to lean on when she felt upset like this.

They made their way downstairs.

"Where are you going Sam, his father walked up to him madly."

"I am going back to New York," Sam turned to head towards the door.

His father blurted out,

"I am the one that made you and introduced you to the police academy up there, you owe me!" his father yelled where Rein could hear.

Rein immediately looked at Sam, Is this right Sam?

You're a police officer? You could have told me the first time we met, why didn't you tell me sooner?" Rein dialed a taxi.

"I am catching a flight back home." She said not wanting to look at Sam.

Sam was heartbroken; He went up to his father.

"You are not right in the head; I was supposed to tell her!" Sam stormed off chasing after Rein.

"Rein. Please hear me out."

"Damnit Sam why didn't you tell me especially when I told you I was raped by one! Why would you lie to me and tell me you had a security job; your friend that died I am guessing was your partner and the reason you did not talk to me for a few days?" That is why you were mad," Rein continued, I trusted you!"

The cab pulled up, and she got in.

"Rein, please don't leave," Sam yelled.

His family came outside including Ruby who was still there.

"Now that is what you call weak," Ruby said walking up to Sam putting a hand on his shoulder, He brushed her hand off got his bag and put them in the car.

"This is your fault dad! I love her. Sam yelled.

His dad stood there smiling away. Aunt Hanna smacked Harold in the head for laughing at the whole situation.

Sam thanked Aunt Hanna for the room, and board then got in the car and made the long trip back home thinking about Rein.

* * *

Reins best friend was sitting with her in the living room making some tea for her.

"It's going to be okay Rein," Charlie said. "At least you did not find out he was a murderer or something."

"It is the fact he lied to me, if you knew he was a police officer? Charlie cut in...

"You would have never gone out with him. Charlie said.

"Charlie, he lied to me though, he said he worked for security. Rein felt a tear roll down her cheeks.

"Well it's not like he completely lied he had some truth in that, she laughed.

Rein was unsure of what to do she had not seen Sam, no text no calls for three days. Was this a sign that they should not be together Rein thought.

* * *

Sam was focused on getting so drunk in a bar in Virginia that he stayed in a hotel for three days with no one to spend it with. He was missing Rein; her smell ran through his nose as he was on the hotel bed thinking she was next to him. He was embarrassed to call her, he had no received any texts or calls, only Ruby's number popped up a few times and he declined them.

How was he going to get his things out of her apartment, he had to see her, but after he sobered up, it was back to New York for him in the morning.

Sam checked out and walked quickly to his car. He had seven hours to go. Wherever Rein was, he was going to find her and tell her that he loved her and wanted to be with her for the rest of his life. He drove speeding until he stumbled on traffic.

His phone started to ring, looking at the phone he saw his fathers' picture pop up, He didn't want to deal with his dad right now but picked it up anyway.

"Son you have to come back to South Carolina we need to talk.

"Listen, dad, we can talk right here over the phone."

"Okay fine then, Your Aunt Hanna is in the hospital and wants to talk to you."

"Put her on the phone," Sam said in a upset tone.

The phone ruffled a little.

"Aunt Hanna?" Sam spoke.

"Hi Sam, she replied with a weak voice, low tone. I need to talk to you about my estate; I am giving it to you, you deserve it, you and your girlfriend soon to be wife. I saw you lite up when she came around, I am leaving the deed to you, I do not have that much time, and I am also leaving you five million dollars for your future children. Your father does not know that I am doing this, and I want you and him to squash anything you guys are going through, please. Your mother would have been so proud of you; I love you, Sam."

Sam was speechless, money was nice, but Rein is what made him happy without her who was he going to live in the house with.

"Thank you, Aunt Hanna. I love you too" Sam finished, and both lines hung up. Aunt Hanna's rare Disease put her light out this time, Sam didn't know it was that bad. He prayed on the way home that Rein would take him back.

He had to get to Rein quicker. He returned the rental to a close airport and bought a ticket.

"One ticket please for a flight to New York. The sun was starting to go down, and it was starting to get colder, Sam thought of the future with Rein and Christmas, and when he would propose to her, that was if they got back together. He was lost without her.

BACK HOME

Chapter 11

Sam caught a taxi to Rein's apartment; her car was out front, so she must have been there. He went up the stairs and knocked on the door. She came to the door with tired eyes and her pajamas on; it was 12 am in the morning.

"Sam what are you doing here, I do not want to see you anymore, please get your things and go away." Rein said angrily

"Rein please I was going to tell you he said stepping in the apartment searching for his belongings.

"Please Rein I am in love with you, I love you so much Sam dropped his clothes and went to hug her."

"You could have told me, Sam!" Rein yelled pushing her coiled hair back, looking at Sam.

She was so gorgeous when she was upset.

"You should have said something"! Rein continued to yell at him.

"I was going to tell you but then you told me what happened to you and I thought you would not like me anymore." Sam said getting closer to her; Rein could not move, it was like she was stuck with crazy glue.

They looked each other in the eyes as Sam passionately kissed her. Her pain was there, and he could see it. He wanted her to relax so she could feel his passion flow through her, he was never going to leave Rein it just wasn't an option.

Rein was picked up with Sam's strong arms as they made their way to the bedroom. He laid her down and took her clothes off inch by inch touching each other delicately. Reins thighs quivered, and her body shook as he entered her space, he was making love to her like it was her first time, they had missed each other and wanted to be one.

His hands gently grabbed Reins hair pulling ever so slightly as he kissed her neck. Sam laid next to Rein in the wake of the morning watching her sleep soundly, touching her lips, he was mesmerized.

He was hoping she was pregnant with his baby, even though he was getting ahead of himself it felt like the relationship between him and Rein had taken on a whole new meaning.

Rein woke up stretching then looking at Sam; he was so gentle and kind even though he had lied to her, Rein could not be apart from him she had missed him so much a tear started to fall.

"What's wrong Sam asked did I do something wrong?"

"No, you did everything right, I missed you for the past few days you did not call me, why didn't you call me? " Rein said hitting his chest lightly.

"Rein I was going through some things, like was I good enough for you, were you going to take me back?"

I had to wait. He continued

"How did you know I was going to wait for you?" Rein asked.

"Because I know you love me, Sam replied.

She grasped his hands and looked into his eyes and kissed him.

"On my way back, I got a phone call that Aunt Hanna was in the hospital and she was not going to make it; Our lives are going to change Rein," she is leaving me her house and giving me 5 million dollars," "She wants me and my dad to be civil to each other." Sam explained

"My dad is not the civil type."

"Rein, I am sorry for dragging you into this mess of a family I have." Sam continued.

"It's okay, it is better than no family. Rein said checking the time, Shit I am going to be late; I am getting so tired of working for these people.

"I will be here when you get back," Sam said getting out of the bed smacking Reins cheeks as she bent down to pick her clothes up off the floor.

"Don't you have work?" Rein asked Sam.

"I don't; I'm still on vacation." Sam said walking her to the door.

Sam laid in bed and turned on the television.

"So that means you're going to cook too right?" Rein asked grabbing her bag and keys.

"Ill text you before you get home," Sam said

getting up to give her a quick kiss goodbye and reassuring her he was going to make dinner.

What was he going to do all day, he wondered?

He went back to sleep and didn't wake up until Rein almost came home in the late afternoon.

"Babe I am home Rein said entering her apartment." (They were not technically back together yet.)

Rein was waiting for Sam to ask the questions.

She put her things down on the couch and smelled something great coming from the kitchen. She walked in the kitchen; Sam had headphones on jamming out to music, he had no idea she was behind him.

Sam?! She yelled as loud as she could.

Sam jumped when he heard Rein. He took the headphones off.

"I did not know you were going to be home this early; I had everything planned out, I was going to treat you to some chicken parmesan then shower you with a chocolate mousse dessert", he continued.

Rein wondered, how he suddenly got good at cooking, it smelled amazing as she went up to the pots and whiffed in the smell.

"Nope don't touch," Sam said whisking her away from the kitchen.

He led her to the bathroom and there before her eyes was a bath full of rose petals and bubbles.

Was this his sorry for lying to her?

She did not know, but she was getting in the bath. She started to take her clothes off then Sam came in.

"Let me do that for you; I do not want you to do nothing." Sam said kissing an inch of her shoulder.

Rein was hoping there weren't any sweat marks on her underwear. He took off all her clothes for her and put them in the hamper.

Sam stared at her sexy body as she dipped in the bath and laid back as the bubbles covered her breast.

"I will be right back" he said kissing her and walked out of the bathroom.

This is what Rein always wanted, a man no matter what color to cater to her needs coming home from a long day from work; he was her king.

ENGAGEMENT

Chapter 12

Rein sat at the table with a nice spread that Sam put out on the table, it was almost like he was a pro at cooking. Even though the chicken was a little tough, she gave him an "A" for trying.

"It is so delicious," Rein said looking at him lovingly.

Sam wiped the sweat away from his forehead with a napkin. Rein took another bite out of her chicken.

"So, what are we doing tonight," Sam asked as he took a sip of wine.

Rein looked at him drained, Sleep," she responded.

Sam got up and walked to her.

You are so beautiful he held out his hand getting on one knee saying, "I want you to be in my life forever and go through what ever you go through, I want to have babies with you a life with you and stay forever, he took out a good sized diamond ring. "Wait pump your breaks," Rein said, are we back together and is this a proposal?"

"Yes, and Yes." Sam said making the decision for her.

Rein thought for a few seconds as Sam waited for an answer.

"I forgive you Sam and yes I will marry you, but don't lie to me anymore, please." Rein said looking at the ring.

"Okay so how are we going to do this, your dad is racist and doesn't like me." Rein reminded Sam.

"Listen to me, Sam said grabbing her hand, everything is going to be okay."

"Tomorrow we will go look for a venue and go to my church," Sam said sipping a beer.

Sam wished he could just get married to this woman the next day. He was so in love with her.

"Now we need to have an engagement party, Sam continued, and we will invite my cousin. Rein only had her friend Charlie and some co-workers that she could invite.

The next day, Sam and Rein loaded up the truck with snacks only because they were going to be out all day looking at venues and places for their registry.

"Are you ready Sam said looking at Rein. "Yupp I am ready. Rein replied.

Rein started feeling a little sick at this point; it was not the way Sam was driving but the way she felt. She could not hold it in Rein covered her mouth as puke went everywhere.

"Oh, shit Rein what did you eat?" Sam asked.

Another stream of vomit all over his dash. He pulled over to the side. Rein ran towards the grassy area; Sam went to help, Rein.

"I feel horrible can you bring me to my clinic?

Sam helped Rein back in the truck with a plastic bag in hand in case she wanted to throw up again. They drove to Rein doctor's office. Sam helped her out of the truck and entered the office. "Is everything ok Rein," one of her co-workers asked her.

"I am not feeling to well can you run a scan on me, please.

"We have to check if you are pregnant first her nurse reminded her.

They brought back a pregnancy test.

Two lines came up,

Rein nearly almost fainted when she saw the lines.

"She is pregnant? Sam asked.

"Yeah, we can check again if you like," the nurse replied.

"Yes, please Rein said, Sam, looked at her, "How did this happen?" Sam asked.

"Well, Rein started, your pull-out method does not work."

She was happy it was Sam's baby but not happy at the fact that they were not married yet.

Rein got up and walked out of the examination room, Sam followed her.

"Rein what's wrong Sam asked.

"Should we keep the baby?" Rein asked.

He was surprised to hear that come from her.

"Yes, we have to keep the baby Rein I do not believe in abortion." Sam said reassuring her that he would be there for them.

"Okay I was just asking. Rein replied, thinking of how they were going to raise this baby.

"Rein what makes you think I would want to get rid of our child?" Sam asked her unsure of where she would get the idea from.

"I just thought because of your dad being a jerk he would not accept his granddaughter or grandson." Rein said with her head held bent.

"Listen when we get to that point, we will deal with it, right now, we must make sure you or I do not stress out but mostly you, we are having a baby! Sam's excitement could not be held in.

"Well, I think we should head home." Rein said taking Sam's hand. As they walked out the front doors, the sun shone in their faces.

A bunch of men were standing in front of Sam's truck.

"What the hell," are you guys doing here, Sam asked them. He was instantly knocked out as they grabbed Rein and put her in the truck. Sam woke up blurry eyed, what the hell just happened.

Rein was taken from him within a blink of an eye if this was his father trying to get back at him, he had a death sentence.

Sam got up and looked at the crowd around him.

"Did anyone see what type of truck they left in, anyone?" Sam said looking around frantic.

Everyone looked at him then one person stepped forward, they got into a black van I only made out the first four numbers of the license plate number. L569... Sam got in his truck and drove to the precinct to look up those numbers and got a hit.

It was not his fathers "MO " to do this to him. He thought back a month ago who could have done it. Was it revenge for Jimmy, his friend that died? He had to go to Jimmy's house to find out. He had pulled up close and saw the black van parked in the back, he pulled his gun, what the hell was Jim's wife thinking. Sam requested for backup.

EVERYTHING UNFOLDS

Chapter 13

Sam drew his gun and went on the same side as the van was on, he cautiously looked through the window, four perps had Rein tied to a chair, she was passed out with her top hanging off. Sam could not rush in, his decision to just bust down the door, he thought long and hard about it.

He heard sirens down the street, the men started to get their mask and got Rein out of the chair and tried to make it to the van.

First shot, Sam took, one guy, went down, the second one got him in his shoulder. Third one in his leg, the last one had Rein in his arm. He put Rein down and fired a shot down to Rein.

That is for Jimmy the one masked man said as he ran away.

Sam shot at him a few times but missed.

He ran over to Rein, she was bleeding, but he could not find the wound.

"Shit, shit he said picking her up bringing her to the ambulance that was waiting in the front of the house. He hopped in the back as they drove to the hospital, with Rein Knocked out, she started to flat line. CLEAR!

Sam was shedding tears as they revived her.

"She is stable for now," the Emt said. Sam wished he did not skip work when Jimmy got shot this would have never happened.

They arrived at the hospital; sweat was pouring from Sam's head as he ran in with the Emt.

He was met in the waiting room by Charlie, Reins best friend,

"What happened?" Charlie looked at Sam, "What did you do to her." Charlie said upset.

"I did not do anything to her, she was kidnapped by my x partners wife, she must have hired some guys to get Rein, they took her, and she was shot as I was going after them." Sam said pacing the emergency waiting room.

"Damnit Sam, Charlie sat there crying, "it is going to be okay." He reassured her.

"I am going to see what they are going to do for her." Sam went towards where they brought Rein.

"Sam is it?" A doctor came to talk to him; your fiancé suffered a lot of blood loss, we are currently operating on her to get the bullet out, does she have any family or friends?"

"She has no family only me and her best friend Charlie; she is also pregnant." Sam said informing the doctor.

"We are hoping everything goes okay so we can have her back out and living her life again."

"Thank you, doctor."

Sam waited until they were done with surgery, Rein was in stable condition.

He was going to get down to the bottom of this before Rein woke up.

He called Jimmy's wife still no answer, he drove down to the precinct and put a team together.

They searched her phone records and finally got a lead. Jimmy's wife was almost leaving to go to New Jersey; They surrounded her house, As Sam got there, they had her in handcuffs.

"You cannot prove shit!" she yelled out as she was being stuffed in the back seat of the police car. Sam slammed the door. His phone started ringing.

"Rein is up If you want you can come and pay her a visit, she has been calling for you and the baby is beautiful.

Sam raced to the hospital and went straight to her room. There she was eyes wide with her beautiful bright smile looking in the doorway at Sam.

"Hi." Rein said with a weak groggy voice.

Sam bent over to kiss her forehead then lips. I thought I was going to lose you,

"Me? No, you can never lose me unless you dump me or something," Rein laughed.

"I will never leave you Sam said holding her hand, as his father stepped in with a bouquet. Sam walked up to him, "Dad what are you doing here?"

"I came to see Rein and hope she is doing well Sam that is all." Sam pulled his dad outside.

"Are you seriously doing this right now?" Sam said with a heated heart.

"Son we need to talk. I must tell you something. I may not be all that great to other people, but I am a human being and make mistakes if this is the woman you want to be with then be with her." His father said.

Something was off Sam thought, suddenly... his dad wanted to call it truce it could have been that he found out about his inheritance from Aunt Hanna, but she said that she did not tell him.

Sam backed away and let him go in the hospital room keeping an eye on his dad's every move as he put the flowers next to Rein said his get wells and walked back to Sam.

"There is something else I need to tell you, its about Rein, Sam got closer, several years back his father started, there was a girl that looked like your fiancé in a car , and me and your Uncle stopped her because she was speeding, I sat in the car as he gave her the ticket, after we left he told me that he gave it to her easy, I laughed it off didn't think about it, at the family reunion I saw how she looked at your cousin, who looks a lot like your Uncle, God rest his soul. I put two and two together, and that day I took out your uncles' box that he had left after he died and found a whole bunch of women, he took pictures after he had raped them at traffic stops.

Sam's dad pulled out a picture of Rein; Sam took it from him,

"What the hell," Sam said, he was in disbelief, his Uncle did this through his whole police years, and no one ever caught him, he deserved to get shot by some drug dealer. Sam put the picture in his wallet.

"So, on a better note, his dad looked at Rein is she going to be okay?" ...

"Yeah, for now, she still has mobility and can walk, I just have to tell her this, this I cannot hide from her," Sam said looking at Rein who was laughing at the show on television.

Sam's dad waived bye to Rein, "Bye Mr. Montgomery," Rein weakly waved.

"Rein I have to tell you something, it is serious, it's about what happened to you years ago, you might not like it but wait until I am finished, okay."

Rein Shut the television off.

"So my father told me about his brother and that he was the one that raped you, he didn't know what was going on because he was sitting in the car listening to the intercom, his brother raped you, Rein, the hard part is that there are other women out there like you; he had a whole collection of pictures that he took of all the women he raped including you."

Sam pulled the picture out. Rein covered her mouth as tears started to ball up in her eyes, they fell down her cheeks onto the hospital clothes she was wearing.

"Where's your uncle now Rein said we need to get justice for what he did!

"Rein he passed away a few years ago by the hands of a drug dealer do not worry anymore." Sam said kissing her on her forehead.

Rein looked off to the side disturbed of what she heard.

"The lady that did this to me did you catch her?" Rein asked.

"Yes, we have all the evidence that led to her she is going away for a long time." Sam said kissing Rein on the lips and sat with her overnight.

HOME BABY,

Chapter 14

Sam drove into a different neighborhood," Sam
where are we going" Rein looked around.
"Listen Rein I wanted you and our baby to have
a great comfortable place to live, So I decided to
get our place," Sam said
        Reins' eyes watered up, no you did not go
out there and get a house, Rein said.
"Yes, I did." Sam replied.
They pulled up to a Gorgeous colonial house in
the suburbs of North Jersey,
    "We can raise our baby boy or girl here; the
    crime is low, and our neighbors whom I met
        while you were in the hospital are nice."
        "Oh, so you just planned all of this
right?" Rein said looking up at the house.
        What about me getting to and from work
Sam, did you think of that?"
        "Why do all that when you already own a
practice?" Sam said as he braced from a very
much pregnant Rein.
Rein started to cry at this point.
        "Damnit Sam Montgomery how did I get
lucky finding you," Rein asked.
        "I guess people change when they meet a
beautiful woman like you that just wanted
peace at a rally." Sam replied.
        "Come on let's go inside all the furniture
will be here tomorrow." Sam said walking in

with Rein.

Rein stepped inside, the walls were all white, and there was a kitchen straight ahead and a living room, a door that led to the basement and the garage on the right.

"It's so beautiful Rein said holding her tummy.

"Babe do not forget we have a doctor's appointment tomorrow to find out what we are having."

"What are we going to sleep on?" Rein asked.

"Well I bought an airbed," Sam said holding her tightly kissing her softly.

"Not comfortable at all. She said

"Also, I bought this. He handed her a body pillow.

"Sam really, you just keep surprising me thank you, babe." Rein said kissing him.

✳ ✳ ✳

A few months passed as they got comfortable in their new house and lifestyle. Sam could not wait to meet his daughter, Atiya, meaning, gift. Sam's hand ran over Rein's baby bump.

"I cannot wait to meet you," he said.

Sam had gotten Aunt Hannah's estate and started to rent it out to rich people. With the rest of the money, he opened a doctor's office for Rein and opened up his own business as a

P.I, while still working at the police station. He was going to give Atiya (A-ti-ya) everything.

Rein walked towards Sam with a smile then kissed his lips, a pool of water floated under her until they both noticed, her water broke.

"Get the hospital bag, Sam," Rein yelled in pain. The contractions were agonizing she wanted to push. Sam came running out helping her to the truck.

"Are we going to make it?" he wondered stepping on the gas. At this point Rein was curled over in pain in the front seat.

"She is going to come out!" Rein yelled to Sam,

"We are almost there, babe just breathe." The traffic started to build as Sam's frustration built.

"Damnit this traffic is not moving," he said looking at Rein worried.

He then remembered he had old school flashers in the trunk, he went to grab them and put it on top of the car, the flashes started working after he plugged it into the cigarette lighter. Going 60 in a 40-mph zone he was 2 minutes away from the hospital, Sam pulled over and helped Rein out
"Please help us," Sam yelled, a nurse came with a wheelchair. Sam followed Rein all the way to the Operation entrance and waited.

Sir, the doctor came out, your daughter and wife are doing great, you can come to meet her if you like.

Sam put the scrubs on and went in, she was light and had red hair. That is our baby he said as tears welled in his eyes.

"Yes, little Atiya this is your mommy and daddy, you are going to have everything that we can give to you, but you also have to work hard for what you want." Sam said holding her gently in his arms. "No one is going to hurt you as long as I live." He continued.

He handed her to the nurses as he watched them clean her up.

Sam went and kissed Rein on the forehead.

* * *

The stitches to Rein's C-section was hurting. Sam came in and cleaned her up and encouraged her to get up, she peed, and it hurt like hell.

"I cannot wait to get better," she looked at Sam with irritated eyes.

"Well until then I am going to take care of you, I took off, so you don't have to worry about anything. Sam said.

Sam picked Atiya up from her bassinet feeding her breast milk. She fell asleep in his arms as milk dripped from her little mouth. Sam burped her and put her back into sleep. He finally had a family, and no one was going to mess that up not even Ruby who was always calling him leaving threatening voice messages.

HICCUPS

Chapter 15

The sun was rising as Sam started the day, with making a bottle and then waking Rein up for work, she was healing fast and was gaining a lot more strength, she put her wrap on for her stomach, and got ready.

"You look so beautiful, in a few months we can have my boy," Sam said rubbing Reins' belly.

"Down Sam, I need a little time to catch up Rein laughed. Sam's eyes met hers,

"Are you sure you are not ready like now?" Sam said kissing her neck.

She pushed him out the way and went to get Atiya out of her crib.

"Be patient Sam!" Rein said.

Sam looked at his phone and scrolled up on, Lets Chat social network, there were Ruby and his dad in a car sucking face.

He wanted to kick his ass, he found it disgusting and made him think of how he could date someone that young let alone his x girlfriend his dad was at a new low.

He had not spoken to his dad in a few days and didn't want to know. The fact that he had his sloppy seconds disgusted him.

Sam closed his phone and charged it and turned on the news.

"Fire in downtown today try to stay out of this area while firefighters try to put out the blaze, people are being evacuated as we speak." The newscaster said as he held a mask over his face. Sam was missing the adventure his job brought.

"Okay I am leaving, bottles of breast milk are in the fridge," Rein said creeping over to kiss him,

"I love you," they both said in unison.

Sam checked on the baby, sound asleep he could play his favorite video game now.

As soon as he had the control in his hands the doorbell rang, Sam got up and looked out the window, he was surprised and in shock that she found out where he was living.

"Ruby, what the hell are you doing here?" He said before opening the door.

"Well, I was just in the area and thought I would come to check you out since you have a new baby and new "Fiancé if that is what you want to call "it." Ruby said with an attitude. Sam opened the door.

He was holding back every strength in him not to hit this woman smoothe out the door.

"What do you want Ruby?" Sam asked letting her in.

"What I want is for you to come back to me, Sam." Ruby said arms folded.

She was crazy she was just on social media tongue tied with his father, no way in hell was he going to entertain her?

"Please leave." Sam said pointing out the door.

"I don't want to go, but I would love to meet the baby," Ruby said making her way further into the house.

Ruby walked fast towards the baby's room Atiya was laying fast asleep.

"She is adorable," Ruby said almost going to lift her, Sam put his hand out to stop her.

"Okay, you saw her now please leave." Sam said.

"Listen you have to go now," Sam was getting anxious.

"I should have never let you in," he said to her looking at her.

"But do you want me to leave?" she got closer to Sam pushing him out into the hallway.

"Ruby, please go," Ruby grabbed his junk, as Sam fell into a trap then his body went weak. Ruby went in for a kiss, just as the door opened.

"Ruby! You need to leave!" Sam whispered forcing her out of the back door.

"We will be talking soon Sam Montgomery she said with hungry sex eyes." Ruby said exiting.

"Hey, babe! You would not believe what happened at work today, there was a low-income family that needed medical attention so bad they needed a shower, and their clothes washed, I am so happy you put a shower and a washer and drier in the clinic." She was still near the living room on her phone scrolling as Sam made his way to her to give her an aggressive kiss. He had to tell her what just happened.

"Rein I just saw Ruby." He said looking guilty of something he did not do.

"Wait, what?" Rein said walking over to Sam staring at him with mean eyes.

"Did she come in the house, Sam?" Rein asked.

"Um so she wanted to see Atiya, he said moving closer to Rein.

"So, you let her see Atiya?" Rein was angered.

She pushed her way in and... Sam was cut off by raging Rein.

"Sam, you are not serious right now? You let that crazy bitch in our house?" Rein went off.

"Listen, Rein, I am sorry, and Ruby is with my dad."

He had failed to tell her that Ruby had made a move on him. Moreover, that she was trying to show him what she still had.

He wanted to but thought how it would hurt Rein, even if Rein did not come home earlier than usual, he would not have done it, right? Sam went in for a hug and kiss from Rein.

"Stop." Rein put her hands in front of his lips.

"Babe I love you," Sam said.

"That chick is crazy," Rein said

He kissed her down her neck, lifting her on the counter he had to make her forget about what happened with Ruby today he was going to please the shit out of Rein. She leaned back in ecstasy.

* * *

Atiya started crying in the middle of the night. Sam got up and went to give her a bottle.

"I am coming," Sam said stumbling in the dark as Rein laid their naked fast asleep. He walked down the hallway, about to enter Atiya's bedroom he was grabbed and pushed into the spare bedroom. His mouth was covered, and the lights were turned on.

"Ruby? He quietly yelled as she started to take his shirt off and kiss him all over his body."

"Ruby you cannot do this, what the hell."

Her hands were all over him, and he pushed her off him, Ruby took a gun out and put it to his throat. What the hell are you doing? Sam asked.

Ruby got on top of him and made him erect he could not fight her back and couldn't believe he was being raped, by a woman he thought would never harm him.

He could not do anything because the gun was so close to his Adam apple it was cold to the tip. Ruby rode enjoying herself. He let go and cried. "Damnit Ruby you are not going to get away with this shit." Sam said.

"I already did who is going to believe you?" Ruby laughed.

"Definitely, not your fiancé." She said getting off him pulling down her skirt lowering the gun.

Sam did not know what to do in this situation; he was a man that was just raped, how was he going to explain this to Rein.

She would not believe him; he went to wash his body off before feeding Atiya.

Feeling disgusted, defiled and out of his body he went to lay next to Rein and held her feeling lost not knowing how to deal with this emotion he had.

He had been violated; it ran in his head multiple times.

"Babe, you okay?" Rein turned sleepy-eyed towards him. "I am fine babe," he lied.

HE STILL LIVES BLUE

Chapter 16

This had to be the worst day of Sam's life he came forward the next day to his sergeant.

"You mean to tell me your ex raped you? she broke into your house and raped you?" His Sergeant laughed in his face.

"Sam do you have evidence.?" He continued.

"No, I took a shower after she left out of the window, she held a gun to my throat, while my fiancé and child were in the next room." Sam said upset.

"Well, how do you want to pursue this?" his Sergeant said sitting in his chair.

"I want to press charges against her she raped me I am not letting her get away with it." With tears in his eyes, Sam let out a sigh, "she raped me, I am not lying to you."

His sergeant wrote down his statement.

"All right Montgomery, I have all the information here," his Sergeant said signing the paperwork.

"I would also like to file a restraining order," Sam said with his head bent.

"All right," his sergeant continued.

Sam did not know how to stomach the fact that he had been raped at gunpoint from his Ex Ruby.

He hoped they would find her and charge her like if a man raped a woman. He finally knew how Rein felt, he had to confess to her in what happened.

Sam went home with his head bent low walking in the house to find Rein in the kitchen clutching Atiya tight crying.

What the.... Sam said walking in more to the kitchen.

"Ruby are you serious right now, lower the damn gun Ruby, what the hell are you doing?" Sam said agitated.

"You are back after you raped me? You need to get out of my life and stay out, and I never wanted it to be like this," Sam said stepping closer to her.

"Get back Sam, you ruined me; I loved you!"

"You dumped me and she, she got my life, the life I was supposed to have with you, you let this black bitch corrupt your mind." Ruby said getting closer to Rein with the gun pointed to her head.

"Damnit Ruby do not do something that your going to regret. Sam said inching towards her.

Rein stood in fear as tears rolled down her eyes, head bent.

"Ruby the police will be here in a few, please, Sam pleaded with her, don't make this mistake." He continued.

Ruby cocked back the gun.

"If you are not going to be with me, then you cannot be with anyone else, Ruby's finger went on the trigger.

Sam sacked her before she could shoot. Ruby started crying to Sam, He raped me! He raped me!

"What the hell are you talking about? Sam said, confused with Ruby still pinned to the ground.

"Your father RAPED me!

What the hell, Ruby is this true? Shaking, Rein ran to the bedroom still holding Atiya.

Sam, he raped me before we went to the reunion, and forced me to go with him, I did not want to. Ruby said crying.

Sam got off her and picked her up and put cuffs on her.

Ruby, you are going to prison that still doesn't give you a right to rape me and then put a gun to my family and me.

"This is all your fault, Sam! If you had just stayed with me, I would not have taken your apartment and or got raped by your old ass daddy!" Ruby yelled.

"Sam sat down at the stool by the high counter.

"Where is my father at now?" He asked Ruby.

"I do not know I moved out a few days ago because he tried to rape me again." Ruby said crying.

Sam called the police to pick up Ruby.

He went into the bedroom to check on Rein.

What the hell Sam, were you raped recently by Ruby, why didn't you tell me?" Rein said with tears in her eyes.

"Rein I was scared to tell you I did not want you to think anything." Sam replied.

"I am sorry for not telling you Rein, I love you so much and didn't want you to worry." He continued.

Rein walked over and kissed him.

"We will get through it," Rein said, since she knew how he felt and what he was going through it was all going to be over soon enough.

The police officers guided Ruby towards the door,

"Oh, Sam did I forget to mention, I am pregnant, and the baby is your daddy's." Ruby said wanting to hurt more.

It took all of Sam's patience not to get upset.

Rein walked up to Ruby clocking her in her lip,

"That is for raping my Fiancé, and when you have that baby, I will be raising it." Rein snickered and turned away.

The police left with Ruby. Sam had to see his father this needed to end, and he needed to know if Ruby was telling the truth or not.

Sam got in his truck racing to get to the brownstone, he better be there he thought, as he pulled up police were there already, and the ambulance was bringing in a stretcher. "What happened here," Sam asked his boss.

"Well Sam, I do not think you should go in there." His Sergeant said.

Sam curiously walked to where his dad was staying. His dad's blood was painted on the wall. He turned the corner to the kitchen, and there was his dad lying dead on the floor with a gun in his hand and a hole in his head. Sam immediately began to throw up. He turned and saw a piece of lined paper on the counter.

To whoever finds this letter:
I raped a whole lot of girls in my lifetime recently I raped my son's ex girlfriend. I thought I was done doing it. I also raped his current fiancé a while back, my brother had no part of it she did not scream at all she was easy, I cannot live with myself anymore and so I need to go, I will be taking my life, goodbye.

His father did not say goodbye to him which made him more upset, did he not matter to him?

He did not know who his dad was anymore, he had raped Rein and his ex, his mom, was probably turning in her grave.

"You sick bastard," he yelled back to the limp body on the floor. His sergeant came and took him out to calm him down.

"That whole time he raped Rein that whole time. Damn him!" Sam screamed.

"Listen Montgomery we offer counseling maybe you should go see someone." His Sergeant said.

"No, I am good, I am glad he is gone. Now my family can live in peace, and when Ruby has the baby, I would like a DNA test.

"All right Montgomery." He said walking away.

Sam was glad this drama was dead. He couldn't wait to get the results for the DNA results.

He rubbed both hands through his head. It was Sam's second year with him living blue. Sam loved being a police officer, but if it came with all this drama, he did not want to be part of the blue lives, he had found the love of his life and made a family with her, Rein understood him after Ruby took him for herself. Rein was that woman he needed in his life; he was not going to change his viewpoint of the black matters movement he was going to calm down with going to the rallies to enjoy his family that was all he needed and wanted. Rein and Atiya completed him.

The DNA came up as his fathers' baby, which was his sister that he was about to take care of, while Ruby was incardinated. Ruby had the baby, and they brought her to Sam. Kayla looked precisely like Ruby. Rein cradled her,

"Hi Kayla, we are going to take good care of you," Rein said.

She started to do her baby smile.

"Did she fight?" Rein asked Sam.

Ruby?" She just cried a lot; I'm just happy I am not the father." Sam continued.

Kayla started to cry, "Shh, shh, Rein heated a bottle and gave it to her sitting down in the rocking chair humming a song her mother used to sing to her.

Months later....

The phone rang, and time seemed to go slow as Sam answered the phone and heard the lab that tested Kayla for DNA.

"She is mine?... Sam said surprised almost passing out.

"We made a mistake with the sample, Sam we are sorry for the inconvenience the lady said over the phone.

"Sam who was that?" Rein asked.

Atiya was in her playpen playing with her toys. Kayla was walking around holding on to things.

Kayla is our daughter Sam replied, hanging the phone up.

"What?" Rein said in a surprised tone.

Ruby was lying when she said she was pregnant. But didn't mention anything when she was truly pregnant. That lying bitch, Sam said.

"Babe I have to put in more hours I am doing a double tonight. So that we can move into a more prominent place.

"Well we still have 1 million from the money your aunt gave us, and we are still making money on her estate, right?" Rein asked him.

"Yeah but, I want to stack up, so we can have extra money, tonight I will be on a stakeout.

"I love you guys he said kissing Atiya and Kayla bye.

"Be safe Sam; I love you." Rein said kissing him back.

Sam went to work thinking about Kayla being his daughter. He loved what he did, and today nothing was going to get in the way.

Rein decided to go on a walk with them to get some air.

"Hello miss would you like to buy some fruit, a woman said to Rein.

"Sure, how much for the grapes?" Rein asked.

They are three dollars and fifteen cents.

Rein gave her the money.

"Thank you," The lady said.

She looked a little familiar and Rein was on her toes knowing it was Ruby's time almost to be out of jail, she was going to come looking for her daughter, Kayla. She turned the corner and started walking fast to the apartment at the same time she called Sam.

"Babe I feel like someone is following me is Ruby out yet?"

"Let me check Sam said going through his files.

"She got out a few hours ago. Sam said.

Just as she was ending the call, she was chloroformed, and Kayla was gone.

Atiya was in the stroller crying. Rein got up after a stranger helped her, she called Sam crying,

"Kayla is gone, Sam!"

Sam hung the phone up and ran to Rein's aide, not knowing how he was going to get Kayla back. He knew her life was in danger. He had to find his now known daughter and put Ruby in jail for good.

CHAPTER 17

Ruby could not wait to hold her baby girl. She felt so lost in jail and missed Kayla; she was an imprint of her as a baby. Ruby did not need Sam to take care of her and Kayla. She was going to go to her emergency backup house and change her name and Kayla's name. Ruby took a bus to Connecticut. They would never find her for a while, she thought. She met a woman in jail that knew someone that made new social security cards and birth certificates. She was ready to live her new life and meet new people. She was in a safe place with her baby girl and was ready to live her life as someone else.

* * *

Rein cried as Sam drove Atiya home after the ordeal.

"She was stolen right in front of me, I let this happen," Rein balled out loud, wiping her grief on her running sweater.

"It is not your fault Babe, we are going to get through this okay," Sam said, holding her kissing her on her forehead.

He had to investigate where Ruby was staying. Sam got in contact with Ruby's Parole officer and got her information. She had Sam's address down as where she was staying.

"Shit!" Thanks, Charles," Sam hung the phone up.

"Babe bad news she has our address down as her place of residence, I have no idea where she could be." Sam said.

Rein held Atiya close.

"How are we going to get Kayla back?" Rein said.

"I do not know," Sam said standing in the middle of their living room on his phone on social media. Ruby had forgotten to take him off her friend's list, he thought fast and changed some of his pictures and put different ones up with a new name to see if she would post anything new.

"We are going to get Kayla back really soon, Rein."

He was not about to let Ruby; his Ex walk out with his sister.

Ruby was going to jail for a long time after this fiasco.

Sam kissed Rein watching her sleep soundly. Her light snoring usually put him to sleep, but that night he had so many worries on his mind, was Kayla okay?

He had to get out of the house.

"Babe I am going for a drive," he whispered to Rein as he put his pants on and got his keys. Sam was going to attempt to find Ruby tonight. He had an idea of where she would be, he'd only been to a house in Connecticut once, but remembered the route. It was 2 hours away, and he was going to attempt getting his daughter back. Sam started the car and drove as fast as he could to get there early morning.

Ruby was in her nightgown as she set a crib up for Kayla and a toy room, her little house, her getaway was perfect. She had everything she wanted. Kayla was her world and Ruby did not feel foul for taking her away from Sam. He deserved it, he played her, making her feel useless. The sun was starting to come up as Ruby started coffee for herself, a soft knock on the door made her stop in her tracks. She ran to get her gun she obtained illegally. Ruby went by the door and looked through the peephole.

"Shit!" It was Sam; he found out where she was. She did not know what to do.

"Ruby I know you are in there, I just want to talk!" Sam said calmly avoiding scaring her off. Ruby knew she was going to go back to jail after he arrested her. She did not want to go she just wanted to be a mother to Kayla.

"Ruby?" Sam said getting impatient.

"No, you just want to take Kayla away," Ruby said picking Kayla up holding her close. Kayla started to cry.

Banging on the door, from Sam, made Ruby jump as she backed into a corner. The door had broken down. Sam rushed in looking crazily around the entrance of the house. Ruby pulled out a gun, she walked up behind Sam and put it to his head.

"I want to be a mother to Kayla why won't you give me that, Sam? Ruby said.

"They took her away from me as soon as she was born, I only caught a glimpse of her when they were cleaning her up, and then they put me back in my cell." Ruby continued.

"Listen, I understand how you may feel, Sam said, arms raised thinking of a way to get the gun from her and grab Kayla out of the way.

"You have no idea how I felt being raped by your father; I wanted you to feel how I was feeling so, I raped you for leaving me alone to go after some other woman you had no idea about, you did not know her as you knew me!" Ruby said looking down for a second. It was Sam's chance to grab the gun.

He turned quickly and knocked the gun out of Ruby's hand. It went flying. Ruby did not have time to react she cowered in fear as Sam reached behind in his holster and pulled his gun out pointing it at Ruby. It caught him by surprise because he did not think he pulled the trigger, all he heard was a shot, the bullet hit Ruby, but he did not know where, as she went down he started to see blood everywhere; he grabbed Kayla as Ruby fell to the ground.

Sam checked Kayla she was not hit. He did not think why he pulled the trigger. He put Kayla in her playpen. Ruby was laying there, shallow breathing. He thought fast and picked her gun up and put it in her hand; she had stopped breathing. He started compressions while calling for back up.

"I need back up please!" He yelled into his blood covered phone.

The police came in and EMT.

"She was going to shoot me, Sam said. He was shaking intensely, that he did not hear Kayla in the background screaming and crying.

He finally snapped out of it and picked Kayla up. A second ambulance took him and Kayla to the hospital in Connecticut to be met by Rein.

Atiya was staying with Rein's best friend. Rein ran up to Sam holding his muscular body in a tight hug. He looked at Rein, with a sad but worried face.

"Babe, what happened?"

"I shot Ruby, she died." Rethinking of how it got to this point.

If Sam had not gotten with Rein, he would have been with Ruby, and she would still be alive. His love for Rein was present, but at a standstill, he could not blame Rein for winning his heart. She was his summer and ocean; he was the waves, Sam put it out of his mind and held Rein a little closer to him as they waited for Kayla to be checked on.

"Everything is fine with your daughter Mr. Montgomery the doctor said as Rein picked Kayla up kissing her 2-year-old cheeks. His life was back to normal, and he did not have to think about Ruby again.

Rein had her two girls back, and even though she was taking care of her little sister, she could not have seen a perfect world.

CHAPTER 18

Sam was playing with Atiya and Kayla, lifting them and carrying them in each of his hands.

"Daddy put us down," they both said at different times. They were a few months apart and were inseparable.

Rein walked in and kissed Sam goodnight coming from her clinic. She loved the way Sam cooked; it was like he learned all for her on how to make the best recipes.

"Babe how was work today Sam asked inching towards her and grabbing her up into his strong arms kissing her luscious cherry lip glossed lips. She wrapped her arms and legs around him, kissing him. "It was a good day babe she said still holding on tight, so she would not get dropped.

Rein was not ready to mess up her happy home with Sam they were about to get married, and she did not want to blow her secret that she had been hiding for twelve years. She smiled at him as she sat at the table with Kayla and Atiya in their booster chairs to have dinner. After they were done eating Rein tucked them in. Rein had to tell Sam about what she was hiding from him. She knew it was going to hurt his world.

"Sam, when can we get married?" Rein asked.

"Well, I was just going through some venues and came across a perfect one; It is in our budget," Sam said putting the phone down.

"You want to get married to me still after all the trouble I have caused you? Rein said dipping her head. She knew if she just ignored Sam at the rally where they met, they would not have been through all this drama.

Sam got on his knees in front of her while grabbing her chin and tilting her head up softly,

"Never say that again, I love you, and I would not change anything on how we met, I would re-live it again and again, I love you Rein," Sam said putting his head in her lap where her love spot was; He felt the warmth coming up.

Rein lifted his head with both her hands. They started to kiss intensely as Sam's hands went all over Rein's body. Her lace nightgown was stripped from her body, and she was carried to their bedroom, paring their parts like a baseball to a bat. Sam lay there looking at Rein watching her sleep soundly, every breath she took made him love her eternally.

Sam woke up to the sun breathing on the back of his head and two little bodies next to him. It was Saturday, and all he wanted to do was sleep since it was his only day off.

Rein was up making breakfast with bacon eggs toast and orange juice aroma. Sam got up and ran for the kitchen leaving Kayla and Atiya in the bed.

He snuck up behind Rein and gave her a squeeze and long passionate kiss, making the spatula almost fall to the floor.

"Don't start something you cannot finish, Rein joked.

Sam smacked her cakes and stole a strip of bacon. He was so perfect, Rein thought. Sam was her knight, and she was embarrassed by what his father had done. The wedding was in two weeks, and she could not think of more drama now. Rein disregarded the thought.

She turned towards Sam,

"I need to leave early I have a special case, he is meeting me at my clinic."

"Do you have to go?" Sam said kissing Rein.

"Yes, I have to he is a teenager and needs help, he has been living in the streets for the past few months." Rein said

Sam grabbed her purse and keys and handed it to her, good luck, Mrs. Montgomery. It had a beautiful ring to it Rein Montgomery; she said getting into her car, driving away.

Rein reached her clinic where the teenager was waiting for her, he was recommended to Rein by one of her employees that said he needed medical attention, Rein saw why. Instantly she had this connective feeling towards him.

"Can you help me? He looked mixed and had curly un-kept hair and had a little bit of facial hair. He was skinny and malnourished.

"What's your name? Rein said opening the clinic. My name is Phillip, and I am eleven.

"Wait so Social Services.... what are they doing for you." Rein asked in horror.

"Well I ran away from foster care, Phillip said looking down as tears started to fall."

"It is going to be okay no one else is going to hurt you," she said walking in and getting her things set up.

He was only a little boy, and she had to report it to Social Services.

"Listen you are coming home with me today okay?"

Phillip shook his head okay.

Rein did not know him, but he looked familiar. She gave him a checkup and gave him some medication, then took him home to give him clean clothes and a meal.

"Sam he is only eleven, we have to help him." Rein stated over the phone with Sam.

"Okay, but it is on you if he is a deviant, Rein you have to be careful whom you bring into our home."

"I understand. Rein said hanging the phone up.

She looked over at Phillip sleeping soundly.

Rein pulled into the driveway and gave Phillip a lite tap on his shoulder.

Phillip woke up frantically.

"It is okay; it is me, Rein, she said trying to calm him down.

Sam met them at the front door. Sam shook Phillip's hand and coaxed him inside.

"Babe he looks pretty bad Sam whispered in Rein's ear as she entered.

"Yeah, I know." Rein agreed.

"Phillip, make yourself comfortable, I will get some clean clothes and a towel for you; Your bedroom has a bathroom in it so you can go straight to your room if you like." Rein said giving him a small tour.

"My room?" Phillip's eyes lit up as he went to hug Rein.

"We need to call social services tomorrow okay?" Rein said to him seriously.

Phillip went back into a slump when Rein said it. She knew how sad he felt.

"Listen, we do not have to worry about that right now just get in the bath, and I will prepare dinner." Rein said closing his bedroom door.

"Ok," Phillip replied and went to the bathroom.

"Rein, I do not know what you are trying to do but don't get his hopes up, what if social services want to send him somewhere else, I see that look in your eyes, and you want to foster him; We do not know his background, where he came from?" Sam said looking sternly at Rein.

"Well, we will get in contact with Social services on Monday and ask them, stop worrying." Rein said kissing Sam and went to make dinner.

Sam ran upstairs and knocked on Phillips door. He peeked in seeing a peak of Phillip's rib cage showing his bones and black and blue marks. He looked down in empathy.

"You can come in," Phillips voice sounding cracked and tired. Sam stuck his hand in with the towel. Phillip softly grabbed it. Then grabbed the clothes.

"Thank you, Mr. Montgomery. Phillip said closing the door before Sam could say your welcome.

"Is he okay?" Rein asked as Sam came down the stairs.

"Yeah, Rein he has black and blues all on his back, do you think he was getting abused by his foster family?" Sam asked setting the table.

"Babe, we will find out Monday." Rein said putting the food at the table.

Sitting at the table was awkward because Phillip did not talk and ate like he had not eaten in days. Atiya and Kayla looked at him as he ate.

"Eat your food girls," Rein said.

"So, Phillip, where are your parents?

Phillip slowed down with his eating and didn't look up, just looked at his plate.

"My mother abandoned me when I was a baby, at a hospital after she had me. I have tried to look for her, but I did not know her first name because it was blacked out on her file, She was young and just had graduated from high school, the nurse that helped deliver me told me.

Rein started having flashbacks to when her water broke; she was working at the time.

That chapter she was trying to forget in her life.

"I hope I find her soon." Phillip continued.

"Well we hope you find her also, Sam said looking at Rein knowing that it was going to be impossible without a name. Rein washed up Atiya and Kayla and put them to bed.

Sam and Rein went down to wash the dishes. Phillip was in the living room watching television.

"I do not know how he is going to find his mother." Sam said.

"He will," Rein said putting soap on the sponge.

"Rein what if he does not find her, we cannot send him back to those people," Sam said agitatedly.

Phillip was standing in the entrance of the hallway listening to everything.

"Phillip we are sorry," Rein walked over to him.

"No, its okay, I know you people do not want me here I should probably go," Phillip said walking to the door.

Sam got in front of him before he could open the door.

"We do not want you to leave, but we need to get in contact with Social services tomorrow and talk with them okay, go upstairs and get ready for bed. Sam instructed him.

Sam and Rein went to check on the girls and Phillip. He was praying.

"Dear God, please make these people my forever parents, and I will listen, please they are so great, they do not hurt me or beat me up thank you, God, goodnight."

Rein was in tears as they both walked to their room not realizing what was about to go down tomorrow.

CHAPTER 19

In the morning it was raining, Rein got Kayla and Atiya ready for daycare and brought Phillip to Social Services.

They both walked up just as they were about to open the door Phillip passed out and hit the ground hard.

Rein began to check his pulse and called an ambulance. He was breathing and still passed out when they got to the hospital.

Mam, the doctor walked up to Rein he is going to need blood, right now we are in shortage of it, so you are welcomed to test your blood to see if you are a match. Without hesitation Rein gave them a sample of her blood. The doctor walked out and in five minutes walked back in.

"Well Mrs. Garnett you and Phillip have identical blood types, and the DNA is the same also are you sure this is not your child?

Rein fainted.

She woke up in a hospital bed with Sam by her side.

"Babe, they said you fainted when the doctor told you about your blood or something like that."

Rein started to cry, "Sam please I need to tell you something." Just then, the doctor walked in with Phillip.

"Your son is all ready to go he just needed a little bit of his mom's blood.

Sam stood up in disbelief,

"Son? No sir this is not our son we only have two daughters." Sam said confused.

What the hell is going on Rein? Sam continued.

Her tears were really coming down now, and Sam just wanted to find out what was going on, was this happening? Rein started to sit up in the bed and wiped her eyes

"Phillip can you wait in the lobby," Rein said.

"Rein what the hell is going on. Sam said.

"Okay, Sam, calm down," Rein said tiery eyed.

"Remember when your father raped me? She continued.

"No, no, no, Rein and you hid this from me, Why didn't you tell me you had a son by him?"

"I am sorry I thought you would not want me anymore, I am sorry Sam." Rein grabbed him.

He gently moved her hands and turned to walk towards the door.

He felt abandoned, why hadn't she told him about his father's secret child, Sam turned around,

"Did my dad know?" Sam asked.

"No, Rein said looking down, he did not know."

"Listen, Rein I need some time, Sam said leaving Rein in the room crying.

He was not going to leave her; his love for her was too high, He just wished she told him sooner. He went back to work, caught in a field of emotions. Sam was not ready, between a new case at his job and Rein's new son, Sam needed to get away for at least a day.

He ended up going to a spa hotel with some of his co-workers. The mud bath attracted some women in skimpy bathing suits; he wanted to stay curious about the fact in what their next move was he started the conversation.

"So, what brings you beautiful women to my mud pond?" Sam said trying to sound flirty. The women pfft him off and got out and went to wash themselves off.

He could not help it he missed Rein and his daughters he could not stay in the hotel any longer, he ran to his room and got dressed running out to his truck racing to get home to tell Rein that he would never leave her that he was going to be there forever. Sam zoomed down the highway. He had to marry her.

He stopped at the store to get red roses. Sam wanted to Marry Rein tomorrow if he could, he realized she was a good woman and thought how he could be such an asshole to her for leaving because her rapist's child showed up.

Sam walked to the front door unlocking it; The roses dropped from his grip, blood stains trailed the floors and a gun laid in front of a crying Phillip.

"I killed them all, Phillip said.

"No one ever wanted me no one, not even my mother, and my father was a rapist."

Sam quickly kicked the gun out of Phillips reach. He handcuffed him and went looking for Rein and his daughters.

They were all in his bedroom, Sam's heart broke out of his chest as he cried and checked for pulses, if he had been there, he would have been able to stop Phillip. Sam cried as he called 911.

"My family has been killed please send help. "Sam said.

He did not disturb their bodies as he balled uncontrollably. His co-worker walked him out and tried to calm him down.

Sam could not live a day without Rein Atiya and Kayla. They were all gone.

Phillip went to a juvenile detention center and was sentenced for life with parole in 18 years.

Sam was alone now he had no one to talk, to no one to tell his truths and jokes to. Just like that, his family was taken away. Sam didn't know what he was going to do for the rest of his life.

He found himself back at the rallies on the black side this time. Just for a little while, he had a woman that just wanted peace and ended up dying because of his father's mistakes. He thought every day of what his life would be like if Rein did not die. Something hit Sam in the head, and he knocked out.

Five minutes into the Rally

"Hey sir, are you okay?" A black woman helped him up as he looked at her, Rein? Was he dreaming? There she was standing there with elegance again.

"Uhh excuse me?" The woman with the blue nail polish said.

My name is not Rein she said with attitude but looked interested.

"I am Vanessa."

Sam looked around confused, the last thing he remembered, he was in the crowd on the blue side, and he fell to the ground.

"Sam, where have you been?" Ruby walked up to him.

"Wait what do you mean?" Sam asked her

"I have been looking for you for hours." Ruby said with a worried face.

"Mam, I found him on the ground," Vanessa said.

"We should get you home," Ruby said to Sam.

Was that all a dream Sam thought rubbing his head as he closed the truck passenger side door as Ruby drove them.

"Sam, you do not remember? Ruby said looking at him, you had a concussion earlier today from playing with our boys today. I thought you went to the doctor.?" Ruby said

"I guess I did not." Sam said

Rein, was just a dream his girls his dad shooting himself?

"Where is my dad?" Sam asked

"Wow, you do not remember anything do you?" Ruby looked confused as he did.

"Sam, your dad, died years ago, he killed himself, remember you helped a girl named Rein to find her accuser and it led back to your dad? You let her stay with your family in South

Carolina?" Rein continued putting on her turning signal.

"I do not remember Ruby, I have to be dreaming," Sam said rubbing his eyes.

"No babe you are not, this is the present. We are married, have kids, All those things you dreamt about weren't real, I need to take you to the hospital, Ruby said

"Am I a police officer? Sam asked.
Ruby laughed out loud, "man you must have been knocked out hard."

"Babe you work at a car dealership in New Jersey," Ruby said pulling up to her apartment complex.

"What happened to Rein?" Sam asked.
"Well, she and her son Phillip are living life in South Carolina with their own house. I still check up on them now and again." Ruby said.
It was all coming back to Sam. He remembered everything; he had cheated on Ruby when he went down to South Carolina with Rein, her smooth dark complexion, he had fallen for her and made love to her each night he was down there for a few years. Sam closed the door and walked up to the front of their apartment. He

stepped inside, to his surprise Rein was standing there waiting for them.

"Ruby, Rein started, I "have to tell you something."

"Sam has been cheating on you with me for the past two years."

Ruby looked in his direction; he played dumb.

"I do not know what she is talking about," Sam said.

"You know what I am talking about; we talked about this before you went to the rally. "Phillip is your son he is two years old. Rein said.

Sam felt a rush of anxiety come across his mind he walked out the door and didn't look back. He had to abandon ship. He could not remember, He was living blue and the reality he had now, he felt like his life did not matter, he walked into the busy street being killed instantly.

Ruby and Rein ran out screaming and crying while calling 911. He could not handle his life; it unfolded like a banana peel.

He was in a better place and didn't have to deal with the two women he loved. He dreamt of the life he could've had with Rein and couldn't have it because he was with Ruby. He was not living in his truth, and dream to become a police officer; It was shattered when he got Ruby pregnant when she was living with him in his apartment below his father's brownstone, the reason why Ruby had to work a job at night and go to school during the day.

It was his fault that his life was messed up. Sam finally realized what he wanted but couldn't have it, a reason why he killed himself.

His dream of Rein and having two girls were just a dream, them getting murdered just a dream.

His mind could not handle his reality, and so he decided to end it.

Thank you, everyone, for reading!

Find out why I ended my novel this way in my next blog post. On www.bluelipsnovels.com

You can also sign up on my website to receive alerts for new novels.

Watch out for the next Novel, Love, Hue

Hue Nelson has problems she needs to deal with before they get out of control. The government has an addiction program stating that if anyone has a drug problem and they get caught they will be sent to a healing oasis then head to jail for their conviction after. Luckily Hue went to the oasis voluntary and healed with the new technology they had in the hospitals.

She has a chance to not go back to doing hard drugs. Before she goes in to her drug rehab program, she meets a young homeless man named Landon but meets back up with him in Oasis, Coincidence? Hue starts to fall deeply in love with him as they start to plan a life together outside of the oasis. What secrets does she find out about Landon? Can Hue escape the sinister behind Landon's weird demeanour? Or will she ignore it?

Made in the USA
Middletown, DE
20 April 2022

64330567R00111